ISBN 978-1-331-51887-7
PIBN 10200899

1 MONTH OF FREE READING

at

www.ForgottenBooks.com

By purchasing this book you are eligible for one month membership to ForgottenBooks.com, giving you unlimited access to our entire collection of over 1,000,000 titles via our web site and mobile apps.

To claim your free month visit:

www.forgottenbooks.com/free200899

English
Français
Deutsche
Italiano
Español
Português

www.forgottenbooks.com

Mythology Photography **Fiction**
Fishing Christianity **Art** Cooking
Essays Buddhism Freemasonry
Medicine **Biology** Music **Ancient**
Egypt Evolution Carpentry Physics
Dance Geology **Mathematics** Fitness
Shakespeare **Folklore** Yoga Marketing
Confidence Immortality Biographies
Poetry **Psychology** Witchcraft
Electronics Chemistry History **Law**
Accounting **Philosophy** Anthropology
Alchemy Drama Quantum Mechanics
Atheism Sexual Health **Ancient History**
Entrepreneurship Languages Sport
Paleontology Needlework Islam
Metaphysics Investment Archaeology
Parenting Statistics Criminology
Motivational

1524743

CONTENTS.

PART III.

NEMESIS.

CLOSING CHAPTER.

Errata

Page 160, line 8, *for* child's spirit *read* child-spirit

„ 314, „ 4, *for* tublmed *read* tumbled

„ 336, „ 10, *for* And, *read* 'And,'

JOHN RAMSAY

B

OPENING CHAPTER.

JOHN RAMSAY.

JOHN RAMSAY was taking his ticket.

It was done as he did everything; leisurely, attentively, his mind for the moment concentrated on the ticket he was taking, and on nothing else.

No hurry nor bustle; no vagueness nor inattention. It was so always.

Whatever he did, he did well; giving his whole attention to it; which was perhaps why he had been successful: as men count success, at least.

For, in so far as getting, in this world, the thing we wish to get, and have always been determined upon getting, constitutes a successful life, John Ramsay's life *had* been successful.

But success may cost one dear for all that; and the question may nevertheless arise—*Cui bono?*

He had done what he had resolved to do; and everyone cannot say the same.

Years ago, when only a boy, not much more than nine years old, John Ramsay had determined within himself to make enough money to buy back the old family place, the old home of his childhood, which had then been sold to satisfy his father's creditors.

He was fifty-nine now, and he had done it some ten years previously.

His whole life had been spent in the effort; and work—hard, grinding work

—had been the instrument he had employed.

As a young man he had given up society, good fellowship, friendship, everything : for his work.

He was a lawyer, and, with the one object in view of making money, he had worked and slaved day and night; never allowing himself recreation, relaxation, rest, or change, till he had attained a certain eminence in his profession. He then accepted a legal appointment in India, and toiled and moiled in the heat there for over twenty years, without ever coming home. His object was attained when he was forty-nine ; but he continued to work as before.

He had lost sight of the end, in his concentration on the means !

Work had become to him second

nature; and the making of money a goal, an idol, a god almost.

He hardly cared for anything else.

The aim of his life was accomplished, but he had ceased to care for it.

Everything was swamped in the passion for work, and for what work brought.

To see his gains increase; to invest those gains; and then to see them augmented by the unspent dividends, which re-invested created an ever rolling and rolling heap, became another charm.

The momentary suspension of his concentration on all this while he gave his mind to the details of buying, re-furnishing, etc., through agents, the family place, was irksome to him.

The necessary arrangements fretted him. He was dying all the time to get back to his work.

If his health had not begun to fail, I do not believe he would ever have come back to England at all.

But India began to tell upon him ; and so he had, at last, come home.

But he had not, for some time, got further than London.

He took some dingy lodgings close to the Stock Exchange, and there he established himself, in company with an old clerk, who had been with him all his life.

He took to gambling on the Stock Exchange ; and appeared to have forgotten the existence of the place he had toiled to recover.

But it was not exactly so.

He had always had, at the back of his mind, as it were, a feeling that there was a satisfaction in store for him in the recovered possession, whenever he should have time to turn his mind to it; it was there waiting, whenever he chose to take it up.

All through his hard work he had always had this consciousness.

It was a sort of vista in the future, in which his thoughts could always rest, whenever he was so disposed.

So it was not so strange in him as it seems, that he should put cff and put off the pleasure of going down to the old home, so dearly bought.

But the day, however, came at length, when he made his long-delayed pilgrimage to it.

But once there, the conviction dawned upon him that it was too late I

He realised the fact that the recovered possession gave him no pleasure.

It was not worth the devotion of a lifetime.

He felt quite out of conceit with it.

It was so much smaller than he had remembered it.   It was a mere villa, as it seemed to him.

Its sentimental value too, to which he had unconsciously clung all these years, was gone.

The memory of his childhood, which he had always supposed the sight of the place would evoke, did not come to him.

People talk of old associations bringing back past scenes and past feelings !   Well ! all he could say was, the place did neither.

His past was a blank.   He could not look back over the dim waste of years, and merge his present identity in that of the fair-haired, dreamy boy who had wandered, and· thought, and planned here ; who had loved every stick and stone about the place, and whose name was John Ramsay, too I

No! He could get up no sentiment; not even when he stood on the very grass knoll where, fifty years ago, he had formed his resolution.

He had not even heart or imagination enough left to be *disappointed* that his fulfilled ambition was nothing to him.

There was no pang at his heart as he wandered aimlessly about—only a longing, a craving, to get back to his dingy lodging and bury himself in figures once more.

Which he did.

His hurried visit of inspection came to an end the very next day; and he left the place and returned to London.

A poorer man than before, for his one remaining illusion was gone.

Back to his absorbing occupations,

like an opium-eater — but without his dreams.

And from that time till the moment when we see him taking his ticket he had never been near it again.

There was another reason which kept him away.

A few miles from the old Manor House, lived his only blood relation, a half-brother, many years younger than he, to whom, on its falling vacant, he had presented the family living.

This brother was married, and had several children, to one of whom the brought-back property would, of course, eventually come.

John Ramsay was glad that there was some one to bear the family name, and live in the family place, but there his interest in his brother and his children began and ended. He had a nervous dread, all the time he had been down there, that some of them might come over to see him.

He felt so entirely out of sympathy with their interests, and with family life. And then clergymen always wanted money.

The church would want repair, or there would be a great deal of distress in the village, or something or other.

Not that John Ramsay was anti-religious.

He had a great respect for religion. He, the highly-respectable, was a man who never absented himself from church on Sunday morning, even now; while that fair-haired shadow of the past had been of a thoughtful, and, as long as his young mother had lived, of a devotional, nature.

He never, I say, absented himself from church once on Sunday, but I will not

attempt to answer for his thoughts while
there. But there *were* figures on the fly-
leaves of his prayer-book, and even on the
margin of some of its pages, which certainly
did not relate to the psalms or hymns.

How far the debasing tendency of his
constant thoughts (for there *is* nothing so
debasing as the constant thought of money,
for its own sake, and the love of the
doubling and trebling thereof) shut out the
thought of God, and quenched the light
of his higher nature, we will not now
enquire.

His brother had come to see him immediately after his return from India, and
welcomed him home with all the warmth of
fraternal affection.

But they had not been together ten
minutes before both recognised the enormous gulf that divided them : the differ-

ence of their feelings, interests, aims, and hopes, and their outlook on life, altogether.

Both were embarrassed and constrained.

The clergyman, accustomed to study human nature, and to meet with every variety of character, recovered himself first.

He concealed his disappointment as well as he could, and did not abate one jot of his kindness and consideration.

He expressed his regret that his brother had no intention, just then, of settling at home, and begged him to use the Rectory as an hotel, whenever he felt inclined to do so.

'My children are longing to see the unknown uncle of whom they have heard so much all their lives,' he said (which sentence was entirely mysterious to John

Ramsay.   He could not, for long after his brother had departed, conceive what he meant by it).

To hide his confusion at the moment, he asked how many children there were, but I need not say he did not listen to the answer.

'I have one daughter and two little boys,' the clergyman, answered.   'Come down and see them and make acquaintance with my wife.'

The last words of the sentence reached John Ramsay's inner ear, and roused him from his apathy.

A lady! an unknown sister-in-law.

He had a poor opinion of women in general, as well as an indifference to their society, which amounted to distaste.

Frivolous, unbusiness-like, talking creatures, requiring little attentions, expecting pretty speeches, offering to sing or play to you.

Inwardly he shrank and shuddered, but outwardly he only looked away, and said: 'Out of the question, at present. I am far too busy.'

'Well!' said Gilbert Ramsay, 'I will not press you, only remember when you want a change and a holiday, how welcome you will be.'

And with that they shook hands and parted: and John Ramsay had not seen his brother again.

He had had an urgent letter or two from him since, on an unwelcome subject; which he had not answered. And there their intercourse had ended.

The visit to the Manor House and this interview with his brother were now matters of past history.

But in the period which had since elapsed, matters had somewhat changed with John Ramsay.

That is to say, what he would not do of himself, Nature had forced on him.

Lassitude and weariness came upon him ; the overworked brain refused any longer to perform the duties demanded of it ; and the doctor, whom he had at last unwillingly consulted, said absolute rest was necessary. Not only necessary, but imperative.

This is why we see John Ramsay on the platform of a railway station, on his way down to the old place again.

We left him taking his ticket.

Having done so, he took his place in the train, bought an evening paper, and turned at once to the money article. The bell rang soon after, and the train started.

C

PART I

ENCELADUS

CHAPTER I.

SUCCESS.

THE train tore along, bearing the silent figure in the compartment, intent upon the stocks and shares: never giving a look or a thought to the beauty of the country through which he was passing, or to the glory of the June evening. Two hours or so after John Ramsay was driving up to his own door. The housekeeper was waiting in the hall to welcome him back.

She received him with a low courtesy: and then led the way to the library, which,

she said as she ushered him in, she fancied
would be the room he would prefer.

He curtly replied to her observations,
and, without giving a glance round the
room, sat himself down in a big red leather
chair by the writing-table, and began to
wish she would go.

She showed, however, no intention of
doing so : but remained standing in the
middle of the room, making various re-
marks on the preparations she had made
for his arrival, enquiring as to the hour at
which it suited him to dine, etc., etc.   His
replies were so very brief and uninterested,
that she was evidently not encouraged to
continue.   It was impossible to sustain so
one-sided a conversation.

She therefore withdrew, saying she
would look in again a little later, when she
hoped he might have recovered the fatigue

of his journey. No doubt a little nap would refresh him. She would see that he was not disturbed.

She had a look all the time as if she had something to say ; if only the moment had been more opportune for saying it, or a little more encouragement been given.

There was rather a stress laid on the intimation that she would look in again. John Ramsay, however, observed nothing of all this. He was watching her impatiently. Her presence was a *gêne* to him, and he was longing to be left to himself. At last she *did* go. The door closed behind her, and silence settled down upon the library, and its solitary occupant.

Why does he wear that look of deep dejection? Why with such a weary unsatisfied gaze do his eyes wander round the room, and travel, with the same

mournful expression, to the lovely country outside the window, lying in all the still
beauty of a June evening?

Why?

Because, as he sits there in the midst of
the realised hopes of a lifetime, there has
come suddenly upon him that sense of
disappointment which had not assailed him
on his former visit. A cruel sense of
disappointment in the conviction that his
realised joy is no joy to him whatever
after all.

He had been too much buried in his
work before to feel it. But ever since the
putting aside of the anodyne of constant
occupation had laid him bare, as it were,
to the world outside his business-room; he
had been a prey to sad thoughts. And
now they suddenly overwhelmed him.

He had never known till this moment

what it had been to him all his life to have an illusion in the future : a promise of pleasure whenever he should have time or inclination to turn his thoughts towards it : whenever he should choose to stretch out his hand, and grasp it.

And now it was gone I That little beacon in the future, that little light which had led him on and on for so many years, was but a will-o'-the-wisp after all, and had landed him, after going out itself, in a morass of indifference and disappointment. Ah I *not* to have your wish is sad enough, but to have it, and to find it dust and ashes, is the saddest thing of all.

He fought with the feeling desperately, and tried to put it aside. He told himself he was ill, unstrung, overwrought, morbid : that the causes of his depression were altogether physical.

But it was no use. The thought would not leave him. This longing to enjoy, what had cost him so much, returned in full force; it was a feeling akin to pain.

It seemed so hard.

When young, he had not had the means of enjoyment; when middle-aged, he had not had the leisure.

Now he had both means and leisure and the power of enjoyment was gone.

That he had missed the meaning of his life somehow, came very strongly over him as he sat. He was at the top of the hill, it was true; but the sun was already setting behind him, and what was there in front? Nothing—absolutely nothing. A chill came down upon his spirit to think it was all ending—and ending so I

How frightfully empty his life was. How joyless! How aimless! Everything tasteless, and now even the capacity for work beginning to fail.

The means, and not the end, were, after all, he saw, what he had been living for all these years ; and now the power of using the means was going to be taken away from him.

The emptiness of his individual life came home to him more and more every moment.

He felt himself to be without interest, without hope, without feeling : without an object in life here, and with no definite aspiration after that which is to come.

A strange feeling of unrest came over him ; a vague longing for the things that used to be ; for the feelings he used to have in his childhood, here ; in this very place.

He tried with all his might to throw himself back into them ; into the dreams and visions of his youth, and the love of the scenes by which he was surrounded, that he might force himself to enjoy the consciousness that all was once more his own.

But he could not do it. He could not catch the broken thread.

The heaven of his childhood had departed, to be conjured up no more.

All seemed a blank. He could remember nothing; could revive no past.

He passed his hand across his forehead, and felt quite bewildered.

A tap at the door broke in upon his reflections.

The housekeeper again!

What could she want, disturbing him like this?

He glanced at her impatiently.

This time, even to his unobservant eye,

it was evident she had something particular to say.

She stood in the middle of the room, smoothing down her apron with both hands, in a somewhat nervous manner.

There was a short pause. It was broken by the housekeeper.

CHAPTER II.

WHAT THE HOUSEKEEPER HAD TO SAY.

'I AM sorry to say there is bad news, sir,' she said gravely, and her kind face was troubled as she said it.

How such an announcement on an arrival at home would make some hearts beat — some stop beating altogether! But here comes in the advantage of having dried-up feelings, and no ties.

John Ramsay was quite unmoved.

His pulses did not stir. His business-mind could only conceive of one kind of news, and he answered accordingly:

' You are mistaken,' he said, ' I have the

evening papers. There is nothing new. The money-market has been very quiet, and there is no change in the quotations either for loans or discounts.'

'I beg your pardon, sir,' answered the housekeeper, ' but it was not of any newspaper news I was speaking. It is nearer home than that. The Rector, sir, is very ill.'

She paused a moment, as if to give him time to recover from what she supposed must be a very painful piece of intelligence. John Ramsay tried to shake himself free of his abstraction, so as to understand what she meant ; and in so doing realised two things : first, that the Rector was his brother ; and secondly, that, that being so, he ought to show some concern that the Rector was ill.

'I am sorry to hear it,' he stammered. ' What is the nature of his illness ? '

' Typhoid fever, sir,' said the house-keeper, in a tremulous tone ; ' and a serious case, I am afraid.'

' He'll get through,' said Mr. Ramsay quickly ; and his tone was so confident that the housekeeper stopped short, in what she was beginning to say.

' Oh sir I ' she exclaimed eagerly. ' Have you heard anything fresh ? Did you know something before I told you ? '

But Mr. Ramsay was only providing himself with an excuse for not feeling, on the same principle that makes some people say, ' I don't think it's true. I don't believe it ' ; when they do not want to have the trouble of expressing sympathy.

' No — no —,' he answered, ' but I feel sure—— I— How did he get it ? ' he interrupted himself, not quite knowing what to say.

'The drains at the Rectory have been getting into a bad state for a long while,' was the answer; 'and are, the doctor says, the cause of the outbreak. The Rector——'

'Outbreak?' repeated Mr. Ramsay rather nervously. For, as she spoke, a dim recollection of some letters from his brother on the subject of drains, flitted through his mind: letters, which, only half read, had very speedily found a resting-place in the waste-paper basket. 'Did you say outbreak? Is there any other case, then, beside my brother?'

'I am sorry to say, sir, that two of the servants have attacks of the same kind, though of a milder form, and one of the children has scarlatina. This last is a slight case, but the doctor says it's from the same cause. The Rector has been

D

continually patching up the drains this year past : but they wanted thorough re-doing, which was more than he could afford.'

John Ramsay turned away rather hastily, and said nothing more. He longed to be left alone again, and hoped every minute the housekeeper would go.

But she seemed to have still something to say.

'I beg your pardon, sir,' she said, ' but not expecting you down, and thinking you would not object, I have had Master Gilbert (that's the Rector's youngest little boy, sir), over here with me to keep him out of the way and to help to keep the house quiet. And then when the scarlatina appeared, it was not safe to send him back. It is a great relief to poor Mrs. Ramsay to feel the child's safe and happy with me. But I thought I'd better mention it, sir.'

John Ramsay was much startled. A few minutes before he would have very distinctly shown it.

But now a certain sense of shame kept him quiet ; and he only said,

'Well, Mrs. Prior, it's an awkward business, a *very* awkward business ; but you must do your best.'

To this somewhat incomprehensible sentence, Mrs. Prior—who, having a motherly heart, could not see how the presence of a child in a house could be considered an ' awkward business '—answered,

'Master Gilbert is a *dear* little boy, sir. I'm glad of his company in this big empty house.'

And then she left the room, and Mr. Ramsay leaned back in his chair. ·

There was a very uncomfortable feeling deep down in his breast about those letters lying in the waste-paper basket in his lodgings in London.

He had not half read them, but now the gist of them returned to him, and they certainly had been something about the Rectory drains.

He remembered feeling angry at being asked to spend money, and impatiently tossing them aside with the reflection that he knew it would be like this—clergymen *always* wanted money for something or other.

But above these thoughts rose others.

The housekeeper's last words somehow clung to him.

There was something about the way she had said ' a *dear* little boy ' that seemed to strike a chord deep down within him,

which had not sounded for many and many
a day.

It was very, very long since he had
heard the words ' a *dear* little boy, and
they somehow fell upon his ear with a
soothing effect. She spoke them so that
they sounded almost like a caress.

A dreamy feeling stole over him, for
which he could not account.

Something from the *very* far past,
seemed to come and lay its hand on *his*
head, and say ' My *dear* little boy.'

His eye was dim for a moment as the
thought of that touch and that voice came
over him, and involuntarily his hand stole
to a locket which hung upon his watch-
chain; and he opened it, and looked for a
moment at the bright tress of hair it con-
tained.

His mother's hair! His fair young

mother, who died when he was nine years old. What centuries it seemed since he and she in the summer twilight had sat hand-in-hand in this very room, and talked together !

He took up the evening paper, but something blurred his vision.

It fell from his hand.

'Master Gilbert is a *dear* little boy, sir !'

All unsought, his own far past began stealing over him with a vividness he could not have thought possible a few minutes ago !

Was it after all that the old associations around him *were* beginning to tell ? Or was it the thought of that child in the house, lying perhaps in the very same room where that other boy used to lie ; over whom some one with the fair hair of the locket

used to bend at night, and say 'My *dear*
little boy'?

What he had tried in vain to do for
himself, the words of the housekeeper,
ringing in his ears, began to do for
him.

Some key seemed to have unlocked the
paralysed feelings and recollections buried
for so many years. His past began slowly
rising before him. He became able to
revive it. It began to stand out clear.

First, the happy, dreamy life with his
young mother, the 'heaven that lies about
us in our infancy.' Then the terrible
wrench of the parting with her on his de-
parture for school; and the sudden going
out of the light in his life: for from that
moment he had never seen her again.

Ere his first holidays arrived, she had
gone to her long home, to learn the well-

kept secret which no one comes back to tell.

He remembered vividly the sudden summons, the long journey, and the arrival at the blank, desolate home—the darkened rooms, the aching void, the emptiness, and the closing scene at the funeral.

And it seemed to him now that out of that darkness and that emptiness he had never really come. All the innocence and the joyousness, and the poetry of his life had, it seemed to him, gone away with the spirit of his young mother ; and, ever since, over him, as well as over her, the crust of the earth—the most earthy of earthiness—had formed. His higher nature, all that there was of the spirit about him, had taken flight with her spirit ; and, it seemed to him now, had never returned.

For in those old days he *had* had

aspirations, he *had* had longings after what was good and true and worthy of a life's devotion. Where were they all gone?

He remembered so clearly how in that first school-time he had struggled against difficulties and temptations for her sake; and the hope of telling her all about it, and the thought of her smile of approval, *had* kept him straight among the many temptations and provocations of the large, rough school, to which his father had, because it was inexpensive, sent him.

He had stored it all up to tell her, and he had never, never been able to do so.

He had come to lay the griefs of his child's heart, and the weight of his young life's burden on her loving breast; and had found that breast cold as marble, in the long last sleep of death.

There was nothing after that to struggle for, no end in view.

He could *never* tell her now; never shew her the prize for good conduct it had cost him such infinite struggles, for her sake, to win.

The light of his life was quenched for ever, and from thenceforward he had been left in the dark alone.

And coldness and hardness and indifference had come down upon him then.

Following closely upon her death had come the break-up of the home, the sale of the place to pay his father's debts, and the removal to the uninteresting country town where his father settled. Later on, the cheap public school, the dull, unsatisfactory holidays, and home became more utterly distasteful to him since his father's second marriage to a middle-aged, bustling woman. Then had come stronger than ever the overmastering determination, formed before leaving it, of buying back the old place some day, the place hallowed by his early recollections. He had had a secret hope all through his boyhood that he should by doing so recover something of the heaven of his childhood, which had drifted ever farther and farther away. After that, the hard work to fit himself for his profession, the slavery at the law, the many years' toil in India, and——— This brought him back to the present moment, when, all his dreams fulfilled, all his aims accomplished, he was sitting a successful man who had climbed to the very top of the ladder. And now— what?— Where was the heaven of his childhood? How was he to revive it? Too late, too late!

He has been buried too long.

He moved uneasily in his chair, perturbed by these new thoughts.

His eye fell again on the evening paper.

He took it up—and the dreams in which he had been indulging vanished, as also the higher thoughts to which they might have led.

The heaven of his childhood departs: he and his young mother are buried once more.

She sleeps, as she has slept for years, beneath a marble slab, forgotten: and he under a mountain of gold. In other words, he is again buried under the absorbing thoughts of his daily and hourly interests.

Stocks and shares! Shares and stocks! The state of the money market! Out come the spectacles, and now no other thought to-night.

Ah! Verily 'it is easier for a camel to go through the eye of a needle, than for a rich man to enter into the kingdom of God!'

CHAPTER III.

THE LAUGHING WOODPECKER.

It was a childish ignorance,
  But now 'tis little joy
To think I'm farther off from Heaven
  Than when I was a boy.

THE next morning, John Ramsay descended to breakfast without much recollection of his retrospective musings of the evening before.

The daily papers had arrived, and absorbed his thoughts. There was likely to be a slight panic on the Stock Exchange to-day, owing to certain foreign telegrams which had arrived.

How he wished he was in London!

He had half a mind to go up for the day.

But no! He knew well enough he was not equal to the exertion. He had been overtired even by yesterday's journey; and he was weary, and unrefreshed by his night's sleep.

It was no use wishing. He must not think of it. He heaved a deep sigh, and sat down to breakfast.

Soon after, the housekeeper appeared with a bill of fare for his dinner.

She volunteered, at the end of the talk that ensued on the subject, that she had heard that morning that the patients at the Rectory were in much the same condition —though he had not enquired after them.

Somewhat shamestricken, for he had not even remembered his brother's illness, he tried to say something sympathetic; and then by way still further to atone, he added, 'By the way, how is the child upstairs?'

'Very well, thank you, sir,' answered the housekeeper. 'But,' she added with a smile, 'he's not upstairs, sir. Master Gilbert is not one that would be indoors on a day like this. He's been out ever since eight.'

'This must be a dull house for a child?' interrogatively.

'Dull, sir! Master Gilbert's never dull. He's a very happy child, sir. Every little thing is a pleasure to him, and a delight.'

'Everything a pleasure and a delight.' How strangely the words sounded in the ears of the worn-out man. 'Everything a pleasure and a delight, eh?' he repeated. 'Now what sort of things?'

'A'most anything, sir,' was the not very

enlightening answer. 'He turns everything into a happiness—like. He's a sunbeam in a house, sir.'

Encouraged by the spark of interest shown, she added, 'Wouldn't you like to see him, sir?'

'No—o—o; I think not,' was the answer, with an almost perceptible shudder; and then, as if to make amends, 'I'm not used to children, you see. Haven't an idea what to say to them. He would certainly cry.'

He ran over in his head as he spoke the sort of thing which he imagined amused children. A vague feeling that you crack your fingers at them, and say, 'I see you! I see you!' several times. How even to address them he was not quite sure. 'Well, my little dear,' he *thought* he remembered was the correct form. And then, if he was

E

not mistaken, children always asked grown-up people to 'tell them stories.'

What a ghastly idea!

He tell stories! With a dried-up imagination and a failing memory!

He was roused by the voice of the housekeeper, who was answering his question.

'Cry, sir? Dear me! Master Gilbert never cries. He's past crying age, sir.'

But she had the tact to say nothing more about his seeing the child. She saw how the ease stood, and retired to her own apartments below, with a sigh of pity for an 'old bachelor who knew nothing about children.'

Meanwhile Mr. Ramsay finished his breakfast, and sat down in the red leather chair.

And now what next?

What was he to do?

The whole long day lay before him, and how was he to fill up the weary hours?

He had read the newspaper through from end to end, and what occupation was left?

The doctor had said there must be no calculations, no brain-work whatever, for at least a fortnight.

What *was* he to do? How quiet the country was! How silent! How stagnant!

How he missed the roar of the City as heard through the window of his business-room; the roll of the traffic, and the noise and the bustle, that told of life's eager struggle just outside his door.

He had loved so, in the early morning, the sense of his own pulse beating with the pulse of the great city just waking up to life.   And now there was *nothing* to do!

Compulsory inaction the first thing in the morning.   A heavy punishment to an active mind.

That lonely country stretching out before him, how dull, how stagnant it made him feel!

How he longed to fill up the great Time intervals with figures!

How he missed the usual absorbing interest of his day!

What could he do?

There was nothing to do but to think. There is, indeed, he reflected, too much time for thinking in the country.   His thoughts, too, were not particularly pleasant ones.   They ought to be, no doubt, but he could not say they were.

Back came the haunting regrets of last

night; the aggrieved feeling that he should not be able to enjoy the fulfilment of his life's ambition, and that it brought him no joy, not even a faint feeling of pleasure or satisfaction.

That secret hope of recovering the heaven of his childhood, why has it flown away?

Where is the light that in his youth shone upon field and meadow?

Where is the glory that used to be everywhere? Why has it departed from the earth?

But he was determined, he told himself, he would *not* be baulked like this.

He *would* have his reward. He *would* reap where he had sown. If he could find joy anywhere it would be here—here in these fields and meadows, here where it used to be.

It must still be here if he could only find it.

It must be hidden somewhere in the bright glory of the June day. He would go and search for it; something impelled him.

Yes, he would go and seek it: it must surely still be here.

He got up slowly and with the air of one who has made a resolution; he went into the hall, put on his hat, and stepped out into the garden. How gorgeous is Nature's beauty on a June morning!

What a wealth of colour in the landscape! What a world of song in the air!

Whether we look or whether we listen,
We hear life murmur, or see it glisten.
    Every elod feels a stir of night—
An instinct within it that reaches and towers,
    And, groping blindly above it for light,
Climbs to a soul in grass and flowers.
    The flush of life may well be seen.

Thrilling back over hills and valleys.
  The cowslip startles in meadows green
The buttercup catches the sun in its chalice,
  And there's never a leaf or a blade too mean,
To be some happy creature's palace.—*Lowell.*

But John Ramsay felt none of all this.

He thought it oppressively hot in the sun on the terrace, and turned away towards the shady side of the house, by a path which seemed to lead somewhere—it did not much matter to him where—as long as he could get out of the sun.

He found himself being led to what appeared to be a rather bare shrubbery or plantation, in the near neighbourhood of the stableyard, reached through a large gap in the tall laurel hedge which surrounded it.

It was a poor, uncared-for-looking place.

The habit of looking upon everything in the light of what could be got out of it was so strong in him that even now it chased for a moment his other thoughts away.

His utilitarian mind suffered great shocks as he looked about him.

What waste of land ! What wretched timber ! Nothing well kept.

Nothing that yielded any return !

Most unprofitable !

The stables, as he approached them after leaving the shrubbery, appeared to be in a very decayed condition.

A little way farther on two shabby kennels, one containing a pointer and the other a retriever, came in sight.

Their occupants rushed out and barked long and furiously at the unknown figure coming along the path.

It depressed him, he hardly knew why, to be treated by his own so entirely as a stranger. He turned away rather abruptly.

He found himself now close to the kitchen-garden, and he went in. He looked about him cautiously, warily, for fear there should be any gardeners about who would speak to him, or worse still, expect him to speak to them.

What a dreary uninviting spot is a kitchen-garden! he thought. How dull, how uninteresting, with its rows of straight green; its endless, uniform lines, all the same colour! There was only one human figure in sight—that of a bent-double old man, whether with age or with infirmity he could not at that distance determine, who appeared to be weeding.

'What a life!' exclaimed John Ramsay to himself.

He got nearer to the solitary figure,

and, concealed by a raspberry bush, he watched him.

'A true clodhopper!' he said to himself. 'A hind, with a dull, vacant expression of countenance in keeping with the dreariness around and with the dulness of his occupation.'

No wonder its monotony and vacuity had passed into his face!

But his prominent feeling in studying the old man was a less worthy one than this.

He was looking at him from the point of view of an employer of labour.

And in the light of their relations as employer and employed, he looked very darkly at the bent, incapable figure before him.

His utilitarian ideas again asserted themselves, and he began to wonder how much he got a week for the very little he seemed able to do.

Why—the old creature could hardly work at all!

There was great waste here again.

This must be looked into He felt depressed and disgusted, and he left the kitchen-garden.

So far, certainly, he had not found that of which he had come out in search. He must try again. He must go to some less prosaic part of the grounds. Somewhere, near here, he dimly remembered, there was a beautiful wood in which he had, as a boy, spent many happy hours; but it was at some distance, if he remembered right.

On the way to it, there used to be a high bank, which, in the early spring, was covered with primroses.

Why—— Can this be the high bank he remembered? This little tiny elevation he was approaching, a mere mound, it appeared to him.

Yes, it was the same, there was no doubt about it. Two or three paces took him to the top. In old days, it was a long and arduous toil to reach the summit. And here another surprise awaited him The wood which he had thought a long way off, was close at hand. Here it was.

Well! Distance, he supposed, like elevation, was a matter of degree; and a child is so near the ground, that things seem different.

At any rate, he was glad to enter its leafy coolness, for it was very hot, and he was getting very tired. He hoped he might find a seat.

The wood was no doubt cool and pleasant. But that was all.

There was nothing of that past senti-ment, or of that old enjoyment that he had hoped to discover.

But suddenly hope revived. A sound fell upon his ear which he had not heard for years, and which *did* carry him back. It was the laugh of a woodpecker.

How distinctly he remembered that sound in that very wood !

It came back to him how he used to chase the woodpeckers, laughing too ! How they gave back laugh for laugh, and how aptly their laugh used to follow on what he said !

He remembered how he used to make foolish little riddles and jokes for the birds to laugh at, and how unfailingly they applauded them.

There was hope here, and he determined to give it every chance.

So he stopped in his walk to listen, and the woodpecker laughed again.

But it did not amuse him now—not the least.

He felt that directly.

It was not so very like a laugh after all.

It was certainly a very tiresome sound if it went on too long.

The longer he listened, the more monotonous and tiresome it seemed to him to be!

And with the conviction that it bored him, came a new pang.

It was hopeless!

To enter into the joys of childhood you must *be* a child.

Stiff, old, worn-out, unimaginative creature that he was, he could no more enter into the ideal world of childhood, than could his rheumatic joints carry him with youth's elasticity in chase of the bird as they used to do.

Hopeless—hopeless! Too late—too late!

His body was tired out, and he was longing to find a seat; and his mind was already weary of the summer sights and sounds around him.

And with a deeper feeling of depression than he had had yet, he turned slowly back by the path by which he had entered the wood, till he came to the stump of an old tree which had been roughly fashioned into a seat.

And as he sank down wearily upon it, on his ear fell, once more, the laugh of the woodpecker at a little distance.

It laughed gaily; laughed again and again.

It was wonderful how its laugh affected him this time. He quite shrank into himself, and wished he could get away from its sound. For it seemed to him that it was laughing *at* him, and not, as in the old days, *with* him ; and what a difference there is in that !

It seemed to him the bird had a mocking laugh, a cruel laugh ; as if it were taunting him with the failure of his attempt to revive the poetry of his childhood, and to enter into the joys of the June day.

CHAPTER IV.

THE SPIRIT OF THE PAST.

Come to me, oh ye children!
 And whisper in my ear
What the birds and the winds are singing
 In your sunny atmosphere.
In your hearts are the birds and the sunshine,
 In your thoughts the brooklets flow,
But in mine is the wind of autumn,
 And the first fall of the snow.

HE remained sitting for some time very quiet, his eyes closed, his hands clasped over his stick, and his face resting upon them; sad thoughts coursing through his mind.

All was very still around him, when

F

the air was suddenly filled with a new sound: one of the loveliest of all sounds— a child's laugh! Clear, ringing, joyous.

John Ramsay started, wondered, and then with a dawning conviction of what it must be sat stiller than ever, and waited to see what would follow.

He had not to wait long.

The sound was followed by light, hurrying footsteps, the low branches of a tree were parted; and there flashed into the sunlight the brightest, fairest thing the June day had seen yet.

The nimble, graceful figure of a boy appeared for a moment in the pathway— just for a moment—and then shot by, disappearing into the recesses of the wood from whence it appeared to have been conjured.

His light feet hardly touched the ground

in his hurry and eagerness. He was in full chase after the woodpecker, whose laugh, apparently echoing his, was sounding now here, now there, now close at hand, and now disappearing into the distance, as if to delude him in the chase.

As the child sped along, he turned his head round for a moment with an upward gaze looking for the woodpecker, and John Ramsay's worn-out eyes had a glimpse, for that moment, of a face which had caught the joy of the sunlight, and embodied the beauty of the day.

It quite dazzled him, but before he could define it, it was gone; and the wood seemed dark and empty without it.

With a dim feeling that he was nearer the spirit he was seeking than he had been yet; he rose slowly up and tried to find the path by which the child had come.

No easy task. Such creatures find boughs and branches no obstacle : but John Ramsay's stiff back was not equal to the strain of such bowing and bending.

However, he pushed on as best he could ; and he was rewarded.

For, all of a sudden, and by a more circuitous route than that by which the child had travelled, he came upon a little settlement before which he stood trans-fixed.

There lay on the ground before him a stick, and a broken water-jug : but with these poor tools, backed by a vivid imagination, what a fairy-scene had been created.

A tiny garden, little grass plots, little gravel walks, tiny gates and palings. Along one of the miniature paths, a little doll, six inches high, assumed the form of a stately lady, and appeared to be solemnly pacing. A tiny tent, evidently belonging to some old box of toy soldiers, together with a doll's sofa and chair, made a little settlement close by, on a lawn composed of bits of moss, carefully patted down and watered.

Not far from this a flat tin box was sunk into the ground and filled with water, thus representing a lake, on which a tiny boat, moored to a twig on the shore by a long piece of coloured worsted, was floating.

Another plot of patted-down moss formed the lawn-tennis ground: the net manufactured by bits of cotton stretched across between two pieces of stick.

Hay-making was evidently going on in the little meadows beyond the fairy garden, for little heaps of cut grass were scattered about with studied carelessness all over the adjacent territory.

Other interesting things had evidently been in course of construction when the little landscape gardener had been lured away by the laugh of the woodpecker, for there were signs of hastily interrupted labour and unfinished wonders.

Long John Ramsay stood there, gazing with a sort of wistful envy at the wealth of imagination displayed at his feet. Such a power would indeed make of any poor spot on earth a paradise. Under its spell, the deserts might well break forth into singing and the wilderness blossom as a rose.

A sermon he had once heard recurred to him on the verse, 'Behold, I make all things new.' Not *different*, the preacher had explained, and therefore strange and unfamiliar, but new with the restoral of the wonderful freshness and delight of youth. Not new scenes in the sense of their being novel, but new powers of enjoying them ; not new enjoyments, but new capacities for entering into them. A world and a life new with the bloom and elasticity and freshness of youth : interests that would be enduring, and freshness that would be imperishable.

And at the same moment, following on the recollection, came back to him the words of the housekeeper : ' Everything is a pleasure and a delight to him.'

' Except ye become as little children,' he murmured. Ah ! that was it !

But how was it to be done ?

How regain what has passed away for ever ? How revive the freshness of so far away a past ?

Dimly arose in his mind the idea that things seen through the eyes of another, might regain their dead power. This child might be able to teach him: might help him to get back into the feelings of long ago. It was a very dim idea at first, but it gained ground with him every moment. It was a purely selfish feeling, as selfish, as it was extraordinary in a man like him: but in his present mood he snatched at it eagerly. Fellowship with the child became a fixed idea in his mind.

If he could only see with his eyes, hear with his ears, partake in the illusions which flooded his path with sunshine; he might in some vicarious manner, attain to the fulfilment of the promise 'Behold I make all things new' in the sense in which the preacher had explained it. He began wondering if he should meet the child again.

Had the boy seen him, he wondered, sitting in the wood just now?

If he *had*, the probabilities were he would have been frightened at the sight of such a stiff, stony-looking old creature. The suggested contrast between his own appearance, and the haunting sunshine of the bright face he had. seen, brought on a violent reaction against himself and his new project.

He turned away abruptly and retraced his steps to the house.

' What nonsense ! ' he muttered to himself as he went along ; ' as if I could have anything in common with a child. What communion,' he asked himself bitterly, ' has

light with darkness? What possible
attraction could I have for anything joyous
and young?'

He entered the library, and sank down
in the red leather chair. His idea now
seemed Utopian, and he began to give it
up. Weary and dispirited he closed his
eyes and sank into a half sleep.

By-and-by as he dozed he became
dreamily aware of footsteps and voices on
the terrace outside, just underneath that
open window.

'But Mrs. Pryor,' said a fresh young
voice, ' do let me go to him. I want to see
him so badly.'

Then the soothing voice of the housekeeper—

'No, my dear, you had better not.
Your uncle is an old man, you know, and
not used to children.'

'What is it you call him? A battle-dore?' said the young voice again.

'An old bachelor, dear, yes. And he's not used to noise, don't you see, and it might worry him.'

'But I'll be so quiet, Mrs. Pryor, I won't hardly speak. I only want just to look at him, to see what he's like.'

'You had better not go to him, dear, really. He wouldn't like it, I am afraid.'

'But—but—' the young voice expostulated.

The remainder of the sentence was not distinct. Mrs. Pryor was evidently leading the child away to distract him from his intentions, for the voices sounded every moment farther off.

Some unwonted feeling stirred in the sleeper's breast.

He looked pained and distressed.

A feeling of keen regret came over him that he had been represented to the child as an old bachelor who was bored by little children, though he knew it was entirely his own fault.

Mrs. Pryor had only too faithfully reproduced his own words to her that morning.

But it was a death-blow to the hopes he had had in the wood; and he gave up his new idea at once and for ever.

The voices grew fainter and fainter in the distance; and silence and disappointment settled down upon the old man's heart.

CHAPTER V.

AN UNCONSCIOUS HERO.

SOME hours passed.

Mrs. Pryor had been in to offer luncheon, which had been refused; and since then all had been perfectly still and silent, both within and without.

John Ramsay sank into a heavy sleep, and hardly knew how the time was passing.

It must have been well on in the afternoon before anything caused him to stir in his slumbers, and become at all conscious of his surroundings.

Even then he did not really quite wake,

nor could he quite define what it was that had broken in upon his slumbers.

It was a sound of some sort in the distance on the terrace outside ; a sound as of some one skipping along on the gravel, and humming or singing, at the same time.

The combined sounds drew nearer and the singing or humming assumed more definitely the shape of a song in a clear treble, of which the words now became distinct and audible.   They were these—

> Fiddle-de-dee !
> Fiddle-de-dee !
> The fly has married the humble bee.

John Ramsay roused himself, and listened with amazement.   The song broke out again—

> Says the fly, says she,
> Will you marry me ?
> And live with me,
> Sweet humble bee ?

'Most curious!' muttered John Ramsay.

A silence followed, as if some new idea had seized the singer, and diverted his thoughts into a new channel.

John Ramsay closed his eyes again.

There was presently a sound in the room as if somebody or something were getting cautiously and quietly in at the open window.

Presently there was a slight 'flop,' as if that somebody or something had dropped down from an elevation and had alighted upon its feet in the room.

Somebody or something was advancing on tip-toe into the room, communing with itself in a whisper as it came—

'Only just going to look at him— just going to see what he is like.'

A small figure; a creature with its finger on its lip, as if warning some invisible person not to make any noise, or else imposing silence on itself; was drawing every minute nearer and nearer to the red leather chair.

The occupant thereof, though fully aware of a presence in the room, did not open his eyes. At last the goal was reached.

The little figure stood quite still. Apparently a minute survey was being taken. Then a small voice said to itself—

'*Rather* like Puppy!'

The figure in the chair shrank into itself. Mr. Ramsay was not familiar with the various forms of paternal nomenclature in vogue among children; and mistaking the allusion was filled with morbid sensitiveness.

This sensitiveness was not diminished, when the same voice, its owner apparently thinking the first impression had been too favourable, added—

'An *old* Puppy, of course.'

Mr. Ramsay presently felt the touch of two small hands upon his knees, while with a deep sigh the voice said—

'Oh! how I *wish* he'd wake up and speak to me!'

Mr. Ramsay slowly opened his eyes. They lighted on the dearest little boy he had ever seen. Two clear hazel eyes were looking fearlessly into his; two confiding hands were resting upon his knees, and a bright smile of interest and pleasure lit up the whole countenance.

'*At last!*' said a coaxing little voice. 'You've come home *at last*, Uncle John!'

Mr. Ramsay was much puzzled by this speech; and by the tone of deep satisfaction with which it was uttered.

'Have you,' he said, feeling he must say something —'have you been expecting me?'

'For years and years,' was the reply.

Mr. Ramsay looked with surprise at the extreme youthfulness of the person in front of him; but thought it best to say nothing.

'All our lives long,' continued the little boy, 'Jock and Mary and me have been expecting you, and wanting you, and waiting for you, and you've never, never come. Why *have* you been such a long time, Uncle John?

This last question was accompanied by a coaxing little pat upon the knees.

The touch of those little hands humanised John Ramsay. He dared not move, for fear the child should take them away.

'And then when you *did* come,' continued Gillie, '*why* did you stop in London?

What did make you so dreadfully, dreadfully busy, that you couldn't come home ? '

A few more questions from Mr. Ramsay : a few more answers from Gillie, and light began to dawn upon the dulness of Mr. Ramsay's comprehension.

From the tangled web of a child's vagueness of description and characteristic inconsequence, he gathered what was to him a strange and unaccountable fact : namely, that he had all these years been to his brother's children the hero of a charmed tale which had fascinated their young imaginations. Nay, more ; that the absent uncle in India, toiling to buy back the family place, had been held up by their father to his little boys as an object not only of intense interest and romance, but also as an example and a pattern of what indomitable perseverance and industry can accomplish. That the children themselves had added on to all that they had been taught of him, their own imaginative ideas; and had transformed him into a sort of fairy prince, whom they were to see in the flesh some day, and whose return to England was the goal of all their hopes.

This wonderful uncle, the owner of Fortunatus' purse, was to be the fulfiller of all their young dreams and wishes.

John Ramsay remembered now, as the tale unfolded itself, that incomprehensible speech of his brother's : 'My children are longing to see the unknown uncle of whom they have heard so much all their lives.'

His heart smote him as he listened, but his hopes revived.

He could not keep being struck with his brother's loyalty to him ; for it was evident he had never told his children what a

failure and a disappointment the home-
coming had proved; what a wretched, miserly old curmudgeon he had met, instead
of the flesh-and-blood brother he had expected. He had shielded him from the
children's blame by explaining away his
conduct with the excuse that he could not
leave London because he was 'so dreadfully, dreadfully busy.'

'But you've come at last,' concluded
little Gillie with a long breath of satisfaction. 'Here you really are !' And the
speech was followed by another little coaxing pat upon the knee.

'Only now,' he added in a very sad
voice, '*now*—Jock's gone to school, and
. . . and . . . '

A change came over the pretty little
face, which quite startled Mr. Ramsay to
see.

It was so great, and so sudden, that it pained him. It was like a blight coming over a sunny landscape.

The dark eyes grew mournful, and were misty with unshed tears.

'Poor Puppy's very ill,' he said wistfully; and his pretty little mouth quivered, ' I don't *like* him to be ill,' he added with a sob.

'He'll get well,' said Mr. Ramsay, hastily.

'Oh yes, of course,' answered Gillie, ' I know that.'

'How do you know?' asked John Ramsay, puzzled by the complete confidence of the tone, and thinking perhaps the child was in possession of some details of which the housekeeper was in ignorance.

' Mother says so,' was the answer. The

clear eyes, shining like two stars, looked straight into his, and their expression shared the confidence of the tone. The argument was evidently unanswerable. Mr. Ramsay was silent.

'But,' added little Gillie, 'it will be a long, long while first—more than three weeks still, perhaps. So that's a dreadful long time, isn't it?'

And the voice quivered again.

'What *made* him get ill?' he said suddenly, looking full into his uncle's face. 'Do you know?'

John Ramsay moved uneasily in his chair, but said nothing.

'Jane says it was all the wicked land-lord's fault,' he went on. 'I don't quite know why; but that's what Jane says. She's our nursery-maid, you know. Is it true, what she says, do you think?'

A long pause ; but the child took the silence for assent.

'God will be very angry with that unkind person, won't He?' he said, raising his beautiful eyes, with their mournful expression, to his uncle's shame-stricken countenance.

Something very inaudible was the answer, but the child again took it for an affirmative.

'He *must* be a cruel man,' he said plaintively. 'I don't love him a bit. And God won't love him either, will He?'

'*Don't!*' exclaimed John Ramsay.

The exclamation escaped him before he was aware.

He had been gratified by the friendliness of this bright creature, and by finding himself a ready-made hero, and this change in conversation was most painful to him.

The pleading eyes reproached him, the innocent words of unconscious upbraiding hurt him.

He could not bear to hear the soft little voice calling him, even unknowingly, the cruel landlord; and now this last shaft cut him to the heart.

Unloved by God, or man. Yes: it was no doubt true; too true?

Meantime, the child's mood had changed again.

His young thoughts had returned to the more pleasant point from which they had started, and he was once more scanning his uncle with interest and attention.

'You turn everything you touch into gold, don't you?' he said, admiringly. 'Jock says so.'

Yes, thought John Ramsay bitterly, *everything*, into something hard, cold, and

irresponsive; his own heart, and the hearts
of others too.

Hard, cold, cruel gold! For its sake;
from the fear of being asked to part with it,
he had brought sorrow on this bright young
creature's head, and on all belonging to
him.

He had laid his hand on a happy home;
and all had turned cold at his touch.

Involuntarily he put a repentant hand
for a moment, with a deprecatory movement, upon the child's bright hair.

'Perhaps you'll turn *me* into gold,' said
the little fellow laughing; as he felt the
touch on his head.

'God forbid,' muttered John Ramsay.

'Master Gilbert! Master Gilbert!' said
Mrs. Pryor's voice on the terrace outside.
'Where are you? where are you?'

Gillie started, smiled, and then with

a merry 'She was *quite* wrong in what she said! I must go and tell her so:' he ran to the open window, and made his exit in the same way in which his entrance had been effected.

And so, in a moment, the bright vision had departed, and John Ramsay was alone once more.

But it must have left a golden streak behind it; for life did not look quite so empty, dry, and meaningless as it had done before.

In spite of the sad thoughts the child's prattle had evoked, John Ramsay felt softened, humanised, more hopeful.

He felt less lonely, too.

The library did not seem so silent and empty.

The bright presence seemed to linger. He hardly realised he was quite alone.

He still seemed to see the dark eyes with their wistful expression, gazing up into his face ; he still seemed to feel the touch of the small coaxing hands, on the knees where they had so confidingly rested.

PART II.

MIDAS

CHAPTER I.

UTILITARIANISM AND IMAGINATION.

MR. RAMSAY descended to breakfast the next morning in a very unwonted frame of mind. The money article in the morning papers did not seem to interest him. His attention wandered while he read it, and he laid it down very much sooner than usual. He appeared to be in an attitude of expectation.

Any little sound on the terrace outside made him start : any light step on the stairs, or in the passages, caused him to listen—I had almost said, *eagerly*, if such an expression could be used of so very impassive a person.

The fact was he had come down to-day with a fixed purpose in his mind, and he wanted to carry it out as soon as possible.

The interview in the library of the evening before had revived in his breast the hope he had had in the wood. Everything that had gone before to blight that hope had been cancelled by the little boy's spontaneous act: by his seeking him out of his own accord. His winning ways and admiring confidence still lingered in John Ramsay's mind; and he no longer felt so hopeless about having anything in common with him.

The wish to partake in the child's sunshine—a purely selfish feeling as it had been at first—was mingled now with a resolution that in so far as in him lay he *would* act up to the child's idea of him; and that the little fellow *should* find in him something of what he had been taught to expect.

How to do it; what to do, or say; how to comport himself, he had not the slightest idea, but he meant to try. His mind was made up, and the day which lay before him should be devoted to the carrying out of this resolution. Of that he was quite determined.

He was going, if the child gave him the opportunity, to put his own life on one side altogether, for that day at least, and to live the child's entirely. He was going to lower himself to *his* level, and stoop to view life from his point of view.

By this means he hoped to enter with him into the enchanted lands, the fairy

H

palaces in which he perpetually moved and dwelt.

He, John Ramsay, had always hitherto succeeded in that on which he concentrated his will and attention.

He hoped to do so still. He felt very anxious, however. He feared so failing in the child's eyes at the outset. He might, for aught he knew, have done so already.

The little boy *may* have been disappointed in him yesterday.

He may have detected what manner of man he was.

He wondered and wondered as he sat at breakfast whether he would come to him again; or, whether, disappointed in him as the hero of his childish dreams, he would return to his own little imaginative occupations, and be engrossed in his former interests.

Everything now hung on whether or no the child chose to seek him out again.

He could not take the initiative.

He was entirely in the little fellow's hands : and all his schemes and plans might prove abortive, if the child so willed.

Time passed on ; breakfast was nearly over, and his hopes were beginning to fade away, when suddenly dancing footsteps were heard on the terrace, and the bright little face looked in at the window.

' Well ! ' said a gay voice. ' Good morning, Uncle John. How are you this morning ? '

There was a tremulous eagerness in Mr. Ramsay's glance and voice, as he answered, ' Good morning ; how — are — you — this morning ? '

He thought how formal his greeting sounded, though he purposely used the same form of salutation, word for word, as his little nephew.

'Won't—you, won't you—come in?' he said; 'or,' he added quickly, with a sudden revolt against his own dulness and formality, 'perhaps you would rather stay out there in the air—and sunshine.'

The latter course seemed to him so much more in keeping with the general appearance of the bright apparition.

For all answer, the sprite bounded into the room through the window, and came up to the breakfast-table.

Seen so near, the vision was brighter than ever, and John Ramsay feared to see it disappear.

'Won't you sit down and have some breakfast?' he said.

He spoke with a certain diffidence and

timorousness in his manner. It was born
of the same sort of feeling you have when
you are trying to get near a bird or a
butterfly, and are afraid to move or speak,
for fear you should scare it away.

'I've had my breakfast, long and long
ago,' laughed little Gillie ; 'but it will be
great fun to see you have yours.'

Mr. Ramsay gazed round him, wondering what amusement a prosaic breakfast-table could possibly offer. He dreaded
the child finding it dull, and leaving him ;
and felt very nervous as to his own powers
of creating conversation.

Gillie, meanwhile, was dragging a heavy
chair to his uncle's side, and was soon occupied in establishing himself thereon.

Mr. Ramsay watched him furtively, and
began racking his brain for something
to say.

'What are we going to do to-day?' asked Gillie, with a sublime confidence that their paths would lie together.

This was beyond what Mr. Ramsay could have hoped for; and he began to feel a little more confident.

'What would you *like* to do?' he said.

He chose his words carefully. He was afraid of saying too little, or too much.

He had not *really* an idea what to propose, and felt that anything he suggested might appear prosaic and uninviting, or expose his entire ignorance of children's tastes.

He wished to shift all responsibility on the child, and be guided entirely by him. His own attitude must be one of strict neutrality. It was his only safety.

'Let me do whatever you do,' said the

little boy. 'Let me stay with you *all* the morning. *Do* let me

A feeling of great gratification stole into John Ramsay's heart.

Something warm vibrated there for a moment, and stole over his whole frame.

It was certainly *most* incomprehensible; but it was very encouraging.

'Oh! certainly,' he said, in his stiff, old-fashioned manner; 'but—won't you find it —rather—rather dull?'

'Dull?' echoed Gillie. 'How do you mean *dull*?'

'I thought—I thought——' stammered Mr. Ramsay, but checked himself, feeling it would be better not to put ideas into the child's head.

'Will you come out directly you've done your breakfast?' said Gillie. 'What were you meaning to do when you'd done?'

Had Mr. Ramsay consulted his own inclinations he would have said, 'Sit and rest in the red leather chair'; but true to his resolution he put his own feelings on one side, and answered, 'I will do what you like.   What do you generally do? How do you,' with a deep sigh, 'get through—I mean spend—the long day?'

'*Long?*' echoed Gillie.   'How do you mean long?   It's much too short, *I* think. Bedtime,' with a sigh as deep as his uncle's, 'always seems to come directly!   Well, first of all I generally go and look for eggs in the shrubbery and stables and hay-loft.   Then I go and see the dogs. Then I work at my garden in the wood. Then I go to Edmund in the court-yard to feed the young blackbirds.   Then——But will you *reely* do all this with me, Uncle John? or will you get very soon tired?'

Mr. Ramsay thought it probable, but was afraid to say so.

The programme had certainly alarmed him, albeit certain parts of it were wholly unintelligible.

What, he wondered, could the child mean by finding eggs in a shrubbery, or, stranger still, in a hay-loft?

Surely such things were to be found in hen-houses?

However, he was determined to make no enquiries, nor objections, throw no cold water, nor in any way expose his ignorance.

Accordingly, he rose, put on his hat, took his stick, and the strangely assorted pair started on their peregrinations.

As they went along, Mr. Ramsay was

conscious of a slight sense of disappointment when he found he was being led by
the same dull little path he had before
traversed, to the same dreary and uninviting spot which had so troubled him
yesterday.

He had formed high conceptions of the
quaint nooks and corners, the cool recesses
of 'forests green and fair' to which the
child would probably conduct him : of
the fairy visions to be realised under the
teaching of his child-guide.

However, there was no doubt about it;
he *was* being taken to that bare, neglected
shrubbery in the near neighbourhood of
the stable-yard.

They were even now entering it by the
gap in the laurel hedge.

His poetical humour fled away, and his
utilitarian reflections of yesterday returned

upon him in full force. He looked round him with disgust.

He viewed with no friendly eye what appeared to him to be a hen, sitting on a nest on the ground, at a little distance.

Poultry were scratching about in different directions.

There was evidently no hen-house at all. The little boy's words at breakfast became clear to him.

The hens, apparently, laid their eggs anywhere and everywhere.

Why, half of them must be lost!

This must be put a stop to. The place must be cleared out, things put straight, a hen-house built, and——

'Isn't it *beautiful*!' said an ecstatic voice at his side.

Mr. Ramsay was really puzzled. He simply did not understand.

'Beautiful?' he said vaguely. 'What?'

He looked all round him with a vacant stare, thinking the child's eye had caught sight of something he had not observed.

'Oh, Uncle John!' said Gillie, indicating the surroundings with small outstretched hands. 'All this. It *is* such a lovely place! and you can do just whatever you like here, for there's nothing to spoil. And then,' he added, lowering his voice, and looking cautiously round him, 'it's the Land of Surprises.'

'The Land of Surprises!' repeated the mystified John Ramsay.

'Yes. Hush! you mustn't speak loud, for fear of disturbing them.'

'Disturbing who?' exclaimed his uncle.

'The hens, you know,' said Gillie; 'you never know when you may come upon one sitting on her nest. You find new-laid eggs in every sort of odd place, sometimes two, sometimes a whole nestful. It is so exciting. All the hens have names after the places they lay in. Do you see that big black hen walking along? That's Mrs. Stapleton. *She* lays her eggs in the stables. Whoever first finds the eggs, you know, they become his own. Hush!' he suddenly interrupted himself excitedly. 'Look! Here comes Lady Henrietta Loftus.'

'Lady *who*?' echoed Mr. Ramsay, gazing alarmed about him.

'Lady Henrietta Loftus,' repeated the child; 'there she comes! She's just laid an egg.'

'Bless my soul!' exclaimed the bewildered man.

He looked in the direction in which

the child pointed, and saw a diminutive
bantam fly down from the loft above the
stable door.

'That's Lady Henrietta Loftus,' said
Gillie, 'the hen what lays in the loft.
Come! come!' he continued excitedly,
'come up into the loft.'

'Into the loft!' exclaimed Mr. Ramsay
in astonishment; 'but—but why into the
loft?'

'We must, you know. The egg is
there. We must get the egg.'

As he spoke, he was advancing rapidly
towards the stables, and Mr. Ramsay me-
chanically followed him.

'Now, Uncle John, come up.'

'Come up—up there!' he exclaimed,
gazing in despair at the very narrow and
extremely rickety ladder which led to a

small trap-door in the ceiling. 'But how *can* I ?'

'It's quite safe, I assure you,' said Gillie, who was already half-way up. 'We all three, Jock and Mary and me, stand on it at once sometimes. Come along. Don't be frightened ; I'll give you my hand presently, and help you up.'

He was gradually, as he talked, disappearing through the ceiling, and his voice sounded hollow, and a long way off. Presently nothing was visible on the ladder but two black legs ; and then even these disappeared, and there was a short pause, and silence. Suddenly a beaming face appeared in the trap-door, and two small hands were stretched downwards. Gillie was lying flat above, holding out the promised help.

'Come along, Uncle John; you've no idea how jolly it is.'

The eager face must have worked some subtle influence, for there was no resistance to the mandate from below; and slowly the cumbrous figure began to ascend the ladder, which creaked and groaned under his weight.

Breathless, and aching in every limb; covered, moreover, with dust and straw; and presenting a most dishevelled and heated appearance, Uncle John accomplished the feat and reached the loft in safety.

The sight of the child's joy might amply have repaid any one for a more repugnant task.

He danced, he clapped his hands, with delight.

'Here you are! Here you are! It wasn't half so difficult as you expected,

was it? Oh look! Uncle John. *Isn't* it
jolly up here? Isn't it a beautiful, lovely
place?'

Uncle John, still a little panting, looked
round; first at an untidy-looking loft,
dark, dirty, and dangerous, large holes in
the roof, large cobwebs hanging from the
rafters; and then into the shining eyes
gazing so eagerly up at him, awaiting his
answer.

Utilitarianism and imagination gazed at
each other for a minute: and then utilitarianism turned away.

'It must be transformed in some way,
I suppose,' Mr. Ramsay murmured to himself. 'It depends,' he went on out loud,
'on the eyes that look at it. My old eyes
do not see the same things as yours, my
little boy, my *dear* little boy,' he added,
with an unconscious repetition, stress and

all, of the housekeeper's haunting words of the other night.

'Put on your specs,' said the child, mistaking his meaning.

'Ah!' he murmured, with a sigh, 'what would I not give for such rose-coloured spectacles, as would make me see the things that you see.'

'You might get a pair in London,' said Gillie.

'I am afraid I couldn't,' he answered.

'Too dear?' questioned the child. 'But you're so rich, Uncle John, it wouldn't matter to you.'

'They would be worth half my fortune to me,' he said sadly.

'Oh, Uncle John!' exclaimed Gillie, 'why half *your* fortune would be hundreds of pounds, wouldn't it? You're very, *very* rich, ain't you?'

'I'm not nearly so rich as you, my little boy,' he answered.

The child burst into a merry laugh.

'As me?' he exclaimed; 'oh! what *do* you mean? Why, I've only got fourpence in all the world, and I owe sixpence to Jock!'

'What would you do with a lot of money if you had it?' enquired Mr. Ramsay, with a sudden feeling of curiosity.

'Pay my debts,' was the prompt reply.

'Your debts?' he exclaimed, rather taken aback. 'Surely, child, you have no debts?'

'Jock's sixpence, you know,' answered Gillie.

'Oh!' said Mr. Ramsay relieved; 'what made you borrow it, I wonder?'

'It was one Sunday,' he answered, 'when there was a collection in church, and the plate was coming round and I'd *nothing* to give. So Jock lent me this sixpence. Wasn't it kind of him? I do *so hate* having to let it go by, without putting anything in. It *is* horrid, isn't it? But of course *you* never have to.'

Mr. Ramsay was glad the concluding remark obviated the necessity of his answering the question; for an accusing conscience brought up before his mind's eye many offertory plates and bags passing him by, while he stood with his hands in his pockets, inwardly inveighing against 'this new fashion of constantly handing the hat round.'

'Well, I *must* go and look for the egg now,' said Gillie; 'but I won't be long.'

Mr. Ramsay remained where he was, meditating on the, to him, astonishing fact of these children giving all their little savings away to the poor, till he was roused by an exclamation of joy which presently rang through the rafters; and Gillie came running back with the egg in his hand.

'Look here, Uncle John,' he said, giving it to him, 'it shall be yours to-day, because you came up into the loft, and so in a sort of a way you found it. Are you pleased, Uncle John?' he went on, clapping his hands, and capering about. 'Are you glad you've got the egg?'

Yes; Uncle John *was* pleased, *was* glad.

Puzzled, he was, no doubt, sorely; uncertain what he was expected to do with the egg which he held in his hand; how, even for the moment, to dispose of it; and terribly afraid of failing, in any way, in whatever conclusion he might eventually come to. But glad, distinctly glad, and

gratified.   That little spontaneous gift
gave him a faint feeling of hope which was
very pleasant.

It was an indication that he was not,
in the little boy's eyes, at any rate, quite
such an irresponsive, unattractive old creature as he had supposed himself.

It was more.

It was the earnest of the beginning of
a friendship with a little child; the dawn
of a new future, and of a brighter life.

CHAPTER II

'FRIENDSHIP OBLIGE.'

But any man who walks the mead,
In bud or blade or bloom may find,
According as his humours lead,
A meaning suited to his mind.

'AND now,' said Gillie, 'we'll come and see the dogs.'

The descent was by no means easy to Uncle John, and his heart, as well as his footing, almost failed him once or twice.

However, it was in the end safely accomplished, and he and his little companion went towards the kennels where he had been so rebuffed yesterday.

The reception to-day was of altogether another kind.

At the sight of the child, at the sound of his little voice, calling them by name, the dogs were beside themselves with joy and affection. They fawned upon him, licking his hands and his face; they almost knocked him over in their delight and excitement. Mr. Ramsay stood in the road looking on.

It was some time before Gillie could tear himself away. When he returned to his uncle he proposed going into the kitchen-garden.

Again Mr. Ramsay was conscious of a slight feeling of disappointment.

That dreary garden, with the solitary figure in it, had become a sort of nightmare to him. He remembered vividly the dull depressed feeling with which it had inspired him yesterday. Gillie must have observed a slight hesitation, for he said—

' Or would you rather go and look for Mr. Hobbs in the hot-house?'

'Who is Mr. Hobbs?' asked John Ramsay.

' Mr. Hobbs! He's the head gardener. He's always in the hot-house at this time. So we should be sure to find him if we went now, and perhaps he would give you a peach!'

Of the two evils, the kitchen-garden was the least, and Mr. Ramsay hastily decided in favour of the latter. It looked to him, when they reached it, just as it had done yesterday: the same lines of green in prim, monotonous rows; the same bent figure of the same old man, weeding the same paths, in the same attitude. He inwardly defied even the child to find anything of interest here.

Gillie gazed round with a pleased smile.

'Doesn't it all look green and fresh?' he said. 'And the strawberries are coming on so fast. And oh!' he exclaimed with a sudden burst of joy and excitement, 'there's *dear* old Thompson!' Mr. Ramsay was left alone, for his little companion bounded from his side. He stood still, his eyes following Gillie's proceedings with wondering curiosity. He watched the child run forward, and the stooping figure raise itself slowly at the sound of the hurrying footsteps.

He could see, even at that distance, how the vacant expression of the stolid face which had so struck him yesterday changed and brightened as the child drew near. An earnest conversation followed.

Presently the old man looked up to the sky, and all round about; the child's gaze eagerly following his wherever it rested.

Finally, their eyes met; there was a little more confabulation, and then Gillie came running back to his uncle, and the old man resumed his work as if nothing had happened.

'What *have* you been talking about to that old man? asked Mr. Ramsay as Gillie reached him breathless.

'All sorts of things,' answered the little boy. 'I've been asking him about his rheumatics, and about the weeds. And then I've been asking him about the weather. He *is* so clever. He always knows whether it's going to rain, or not, and he is hardly ever wrong. We call him "Old Weatherwise," but his real name is Thompson.'

'And what does he say about the weather?' asked Mr. Ramsay.

'He says,' answered Gillie, 'that he thinks it will be showery, but it won't rain.

So now we shall see if it comes true. But Uncle John, why *didn't* you come and talk to him? He *is* such a dear old man, and I am sure he would like to know you so much. Isn't it a pity he has such bad rheumatics that he can't hold himself up. Sometimes he can hardly work a bit, poor old fellow! He always comes and *tries*, you know, but half the time his back is so bad he has to give it up, and rest.'

'Ha!' muttered Mr. Ramsay. 'Just what I imagined!'

'Mr. Hobbs *finds* him jobs, don't you know,' continued Gillie, lowering his voice, and speaking confidently; 'it's a sort of *excuse*, you see, he says, for giving him wages. It *is* kind of Mr. Hobbs, isn't it?'

'Oh, very!' said Mr. Ramsay, hastily, seeing Gillie expected an answer.

'Of course old Thompson doesn't *know*

that,' resumed Gillie. 'It would never do to let him know, would it? It would hurt his feelings, Mr. Hobbs says.'

'Why doesn't he go into the workhouse?' asked Mr. Ramsay abruptly, his feelings for the moment getting the better of him.

Fortunately for his credit, Gillie misunderstood him, and thought he was referring to an almshouse for the 'aged poor' there was in the village.

'He's not old enough,' answered Gillie, 'not near old enough; you must be past eighty, I think, or nearly a hundred, to go there. Thompson is not so very old, you know, Uncle John. It's the rheumatics that make him so old-looking, and having no teeth.'

'Has he no teeth? said Mr. Ramsay.

'Not one,' said Gillie, 'nothing but gums!'

'How's that?'

'I asked him about it once,' replied the child, 'and he said he thought it was "because he had neglected to have them out when he was young." *Will* you come into the wood now, and see my little garden?'

Mr. Ramsay gladly assented. That little fairy settlement still lingered in his mind's eye, and he longed to see it again.

So they strolled along till they came to the wood, and, entering its cool recesses, found their way to the little garden.

It wasn't half finished, Gillie said, not half.

He wanted to make a rockery, and a grotto. Would Uncle John help him to collect the stones? Yes. Uncle John would do anything that was required of him. And for half an hour did the said

Uncle John go about, bent double, picking up all the small stones he could find, and submitting them to the criticism of the little architect.

When both employer and employed were tired out, they wandered on into the wood, till they reached the seat John Ramsay had occupied yesterday. There they sat, listening to the woodpecker, who was laughing as gaily as ever; but who had already lost the mocking tone in his laugh, which had so affected John Ramsay yesterday. For, with this bright child at his side, with the sense of growing friendship in his heart, he could defy the bird to say he had failed to revive the joys of childhood, or was out of harmony with the bright June day.

'Tell me a story,' said little Gillie presently.

'I!' exclaimed Mr. Ramsay; '*I* can't tell stories, child.   My stories,' with a sigh, ' would be very dull ones, I am afraid.'

' Oh, try!' said Gillie eagerly. 'Do try!'

Mr. Ramsay's heart sank.   Memory brought up nothing to his mind.   Imagination he had none whatever.

'Take me to see something else instead,' he said.

So his little guide took him to see the fairy rings in the meadow, and then to pay a visit to the old well in another wood beyond.

They leant over it together for a few minutes, and then Gillie fetched a cup, hidden under some shrubs hard by, and filled it to the brim.

Uncle John saw his fate before him—a large draught of cold water which he was expected to quaff.

'The sweetest and most famous water in all the country round,' the little cup-bearer assured him, with grave earnest eyes fixed upon him as he drank.

Then they wandered on through the scented lime avenue to the old flower-garden.

A picturesque old place, with its high yew hedges cut into curious shapes, its long grass terraces, and beds full of old-fashioned flowers.

In the middle of the flower-beds stood an ancient sun-dial.

When they reached this spot, Mr. Ramsay fell suddenly into a fit of abstraction.

He stood quite still gazing out into the distance.

From across the waste of years lying behind him, a breath of the past seemed

K

to come to him. Something in his surroundings spoke to him dimly of days
gone by.

Gillie, childlike, did not notice how
thoughtful his uncle had become.

He got up on the top of the sun-dial,
and sat there, swinging his legs backwards
and forwards, and humming a little song to
himself.

' Oh, how I wish you could tell stories !'
he said presently, with a deep sigh.

There was a moment's silence, and then
suddenly, Uncle John, speaking half to
himself and half to the little boy, began
to tell a story so life-like and so real that
Gillie listened to it spell-bound, his eyes
fixed upon his uncle's averted face.

Minute after minute flew by ; and still
Uncle John went on telling, and still Gillie
listened, fascinated, to that wonderful story.

It was the story of a little boy's last day with his mother before he went to school; and of all that they had done and said and talked over together as they wandered about the livelong day: of the promises the child had made her as they stood in the twilight, by an old sun-dial, as the close of that day drew near.

Then Uncle John's voice grew very low.

'I cannot tell you the rest,' he said, ' for the end of that story is very sad. . . .'

'Oh! make it end happily,' said Gillie eagerly. 'I don't like stories to end sadly. I like them always to turn out well. Do end it happily, *do*!'

'Ah,' said Mr. Ramsay slowly, 'I wish I could! I wish I could!'

'Was there a picture to the story?' Gillie asked presently, rather awed by his uncle's manner.

'Yes,' said Mr. Ramsay, looking away, 'a picture of the boy and his mother, standing by the sun-dial. She, young and fair and smiling . . . the boy has the picture still. And under the picture, when he sees it, is written " Broken Vows " ! '

'You're getting *dreadfully* sad, Uncle John,' said Gillie pathetically; 'what is the matter? And you've not finished the story.'

Uncle John shook himself free of his abstraction with an effort.

'Before they went home that evening,' he said, 'they spelt over together the almost worn-out inscription which was round the sun-dial they were standing by. He was too young to understand it; but she told him that some day he would know well enough what it meant. And so he did.'

'How very funny!' said Gillie, eagerly jumping down from his seat; 'for there is a worn-out inscription on this sun-dial too. Often and often we've wanted to make it out, but it's too much worn away. Puppy always told us that when you came home from India you would perhaps be able to tell us what it was. Do you think you can remember it, Uncle John?'

Uncle John shook his head.

'Very little,' he answered; 'a line or two might come back to me. The *sense* of it I remember, but you would be too young to understand.'

'Like the boy in the story,' said Gillie, delighted at the coincidence. 'But tell me what you remember, Uncle John, for you know *his* mother said he would know some day what it meant. So, perhaps, *I* shall, too.'

'It was something like this,' said Mr. Ramsay thoughtfully—

'Time flies, they say ; in truth it is not so.
Time *stays* . . . . *we* go.'

'No, I don't understand it a bit,' said Gillie, shaking his head. 'I must wait, I suppose, like him, till I am older. But, Uncle John, how could you say you didn't tell stories well ? You tell them *beautifully.* You must tell me another some day.'

'Ah, child !' said Uncle John, 'that is the only story I shall ever be able to tell you ! And I don't suppose, either, that I shall *ever* be able to tell it again !'

'I'm getting hungry,' said Gillie ; 'let us see what time it is.'

'It is nearly one o'clock,' said Mr. Ramsay, looking at the dial ; 'how quickly the morning has gone !' he added in astonishment.

'You said the day was too long at breakfast,' said Gillie triumphantly. 'You see it's very short. I told you so!'

Mr. Ramsay smiled, but said nothing.

'But if it's nearly one, I ought to be going home to my dinner,' said Gillie.

'Come along,' said his uncle, and they took their way to the house.

'I must feed the blackbirds first though,' said Gillie; 'will you come with me to the court-yard? We shall find Edmund waiting.'

But here Mr. Ramsay demurred. This dual companionship was very delightful, but a third, in the person of a young foot-man, was another matter altogether.

'I'm rather tired,' he said hesitatingly; 'so I think I'll go in and rest a bit.'

They parted at the door, Gillie disap-pearing in the direction of the offices, and

Mr. Ramsay returning to his red leather chair.

The next few hours seemed wonderfully long to Mr. Ramsay.

He caught himself looking at his watch more than once; and wondering what the child was about. He must, he said to himself, have long ere this have finished his dinner. Would he return to him or not?

He found himself constantly looking towards the door, or towards the open window, hoping every minute the little figure might come in sight.

He was conscious of a pang of disappointment when the time went on, and nothing happened.

'It is quite natural,' he said to himself; 'of course he has many amusements, and plenty of little occupations.'

But something very like a sigh escaped him all the same.

The afternoon was very hot.

Mrs. Pryor came in, on some pretext or other: and in an off-hand, would-be-indifferent tone, Mr. Ramsay inquired of her what the child generally did with himself at this hour. Her answer was not re-assuring. Gillie appeared to have so many irons in the fire; and, moreover, so many willing companions, that there certainly was not much necessity for *him*.

'He might,' Mrs. Pryor said, 'be helping the gardener to pick the fruit for dessert, or he might be in the court yard with the footman, looking after the blackbirds they were bringing up together.'

By-and-by he would very likely look into the kitchen, to see the cooking, or to help to shell the peas.

'Master Gilbert was never at any loss,' she said, with a smile, 'and every servant, both inside and outside the house, was his friend.'

After this, Mr. Ramsay felt more depressed than ever : and gave himself up to an afternoon-nap.

When he awoke, it was half-past four, and there was still no sign of the child.

It was raining a little, and the garden outside looked damp and dull.

After this, Mr. Ramsay 'gave it up' altogether.

The case was clear. The child did not care for his society after all.

He felt in his heart a dull sense of failure and disappointment.

'It is *quite* natural,' he said to himself again, ' *quite*.'

He got up, and walked to the window with a sigh.

To his surprise, curled up in the window-seat, very quiet and doing nothing, was the object of his reflection.

The truth was that Gillie, when he had gone through his little programme, had returned to seek his uncle· but finding him asleep, had relapsed into dulness, which had been followed by a fit of home-sickness.

Mr. Ramsay, bending over him, extracted that he was ' so unhappy and wretchable, that he didn't know what to do'; that he was 'so dull all by himself, with no one to play with'; and that he wanted to go home very badly.

Mr. Ramsay was surprised to find how hurt he was that it should be so.

Further enquiries elicited that he

'couldn't bear Puppy to be so ill'; and that he 'couldn't help crying whenever he thought of it.'

This speech brought a strange pang to the heart of his questioner.

He was seized with such a dread of the return of last night's conversation on this subject; with such a shrinking from the allusions to the 'cruel landlord' which he feared *might* follow, that he felt he must do something at once to divert the child's thoughts.

'Can't *I* play with you?' he said, rather nervously.

'You see it's a nice romping game I should like,' said Gillie pathetically; 'and you can't play those sort of games, *can* you?'

Mr. Ramsay admitted with a sigh that it was too true.

'But,' he added hesitatingly, 'I can *try*, if you like.'

The child's joy and gratitude were so unfeigned that Mr. Ramsay felt himself well repaid for the painful effort which the game of romps that followed cost him.

Mrs. Pryor, coming in to call Gillie to his tea in the middle of the somewhat riotous proceedings, could hardly believe her eyes; and Mr. Ramsay looked rather shame-faced at being caught in the act. 'The child seemed a little dull,' he said apologetically.

And thus John Ramsay received his first lesson in a, to him, new truth. Though his limbs ached, and his head was rather muzzy, he enjoyed, as he leaned back exhausted, in his chair, a feeling of satisfaction in having ministered to another; and the idea that it is more blessed

to give than to receive, entered, for the first
time, into his utilitarian mind.

'You'll come back,' he had said almost
imploringly to Gillie, before Mrs. Pryor
had borne him away.

And Gillie had begged to be allowed to
sit up to late dinner with him: not to eat
any himself, he had explained, but to see
him eat it.

Mrs. Pryor, when appealed to, had
given leave: and Mr. Ramsay felt there
was thus still something left to look forward to.

CHAPTER III.

WHEREIN THEY DIFFERED.

Dark is the world to thee: thyself art the reason why.

'THE dressing-bell is just going to ring,' said a gay voice about an hour and a half later, 'when are you going up to dress?'

'I'll go at once,' said Mr. Ramsay, rising with unusual alacrity.

'And *may* I come and help you?' said Gillie, 'I always go up with Puppy.'

Mr. Ramsay readily assented, and the two ascended the stairs together to the bedroom. Here was a perfectly new field of delight and discovery.

Gillie wandered about in ecstasy at the

sight of so many things he had never seen before.

Mr. Ramsay was astonished and puzzled at the child's interest in all the ordinary paraphernalia of a dressing-table.

He was an unobservant man, and took very little interest in the neuter gender. He could not understand Gillie's excitement over the trifles lying about, nor answer half the questions he kept eagerly asking.

He knew but little about the details of his possessions. There they were; there they had always been. He did not remember, even if he had ever known, how the divers familiar objects had originally found their way to him.

The eager enquiries: Where *did* you get this? Oh! *who* gave you this?—were most puzzling to him. He tried feebly to satisfy the child's thirst for information, but his answers were not very satisfactory.

An exclamation of delight broke in upon his endeavours.

' Oh, Uncle John ! What a *darling* ! '

' Hey ! ' exclaimed Mr. Ramsay, startled, ' something alive ? What in the world is it ? '

' Oh, Uncle John ! Such a darling, darling, little pill-box. Look here ! Oh what tiny, weeny little thing ! '

' Good gracious, child ! ' exclaimed his uncle. ' Have you never seen a pill-box before ? '

' Oh ! not one like this. Puppy's are much bigger and hold a lot. Not like this dear little thing. Oh *may* I have it, if you've quite done with it ? '

Mr. Ramsay sighed as he acceded to the request. He was wishing he had such eager wishes ; so easy of gratification.

L

Another shout. 'Here's just the very thing I want for my boat. *May* I have it?'

'What next?' thought Uncle John, as an old bit of string was brought up to him.

The dinner-bell brought Gillie's researches to an end; and he and Mr. Ramsay descended to the dining-room.

He had been in and out of the kitchen a good deal during the afternoon, watching the dinner being cooked; and had been overcome with the sumptuousness of the preparations, and the painstaking of the cook. Especially had he been entranced by a very elaborate pudding: the like of which he had never before beheld: and which in his eyes was a work of art of an almost transcendent nature.

He was thinking about it all through dinner, looking for it, expecting it: and as the moment drew near when its appearance was due, his excitement grew great.

Therefore, when the said pudding—more beautiful than ever now that it was 'dished up,' really came in sight, and on being handed in all its glory to Mr. Ramsay, was received with a cold shake of the head, and taken out of the room almost as soon as it had appeared—poor Gillie first started, and then uttered an exclamation of dismay.

'Oh, Uncle John!' he said, but he got no farther.

Mr. Ramsay looked round, and, to his horror, saw that Gillie's eyes were full of tears.

'What is the matter?' he asked anxiously.

'Oh, Uncle John! Poor cook will be so disappointed; and she *did* take such pains.'

'My dear child, I never eat sweets. I will tell the housekeeper to-morrow she need never send up any.'

'Oh, Uncle John! *Please* don't: she will be so unhappy. She thought you would like them so much. And she has bought a cookery book with her *own* money, because she was afraid she had rather forgotten her puddings and she wanted to teach cook some. We chose this one out of it. And you sent it away so quickly, *just* as I was going to explain to you how the lovely pink and white icing is done. And you hadn't half looked at all the hundreds and thousands on the top. I scattered most of them on myself. Oh! *won't* you send for it back again? Do, do.'

Mr. Ramsay resigned himself to his fate. 'Bring back that pudding,' he said,

when the butler came in again; and to
Gillie's joy and satisfaction, the magnificent
erection reappeared.

Mr. Ramsay was beginning to get very
nervous as to what further gastronomic
performances would be expected of him.
The bill of fare told him that there was
some toasted cheese next in order; a thing
which he *knew* if he indulged in it would
bring a certain nightmare and hours of
sleeplessness. But the anxious brown eyes
fixed upon him, when the dish was handed
to him, influenced him even more than did
that dismal prospect; and he helped himself without hesitation.

He distinctly, however, drew a line at
cheese and radishes which now followed.
Here, at any rate, he felt he would not be
failing in the child's estimation by doing
violence to the feelings of the cook.

She had had nothing, at any rate, to do with the preparation of *this* course.

But he soon saw he had made a *faux pas*.

Gillie was very quiet and decidedly downcast after the rejection of the course, so much so that as soon as the servants had gone Mr. Ramsay questioned him timidly as to the cause of his depression.

'I thought poor Edmund looked so disappointed,' said Gillie; 'he took such pains to get it all ready. I helped him. You can't think what a time it took.'

'What could I do?' said Mr. Ramsay nervously. 'I couldn't eat cheese *twice* over, you know. But another time when there is not any toasted cheese, I——'

'I think it must be so sad for a footman,' said Gillie, 'at a dinner party when everybody says no to the dish he is handing. He is left standing there with his dish not touched. It seems so unkind. When I am grown up I shall always take *everything* that is handed to me.'

'It would make you very ill,' said his practical uncle.

'Well, anyhow, I should say, " No thank you !" very kindly, and not just shake my head, or give the dish a little push, as some people do.'

The servants now returned, and Mr. Ramsay glanced with uneasiness at the display of fruit which was being placed on the table.

It was a terrible time of year for any one who dared not indulge in it.

Not only were strawberries and rasp-berries in full swing, but there were early peaches and nectarines from the hot-houses.

Mr. Ramsay gave a despairing look at the dish in front of him, and wondered if

he must sacrifice himself yet further
to retain the good opinion of his little
companion.

The gardener, he had no doubt, had
'feelings' as well as the cook and the footman; and he remembered with a pang,
that Mrs. Pryor had mentioned him as one
of Gillie's great friends, and had even said
something about his being then engaged in
'helping him to pick the fruit for dessert.'
The position was becoming desperate. A
happy thought struck him to try what
taking the child into his confidence might
do to keep him out of his difficulty. He
was a tender-hearted, sympathetic little
fellow, he reflected, and would probably understand and enter into his feelings. 'You
see, my dear,' he said, 'I'm rather an invalid
just now, and have to be very careful what
I eat. I am under the doctor's orders, and

certain things he forbids altogether, of which fruit is one.'

'What's the matter with you?' asked Gillie.

'It's rather difficult to explain,' answered Mr. Ramsay; 'but I'm altogether broken-down and out of sorts, and feel ill and wretched.'

'Oh, Uncle John!' exclaimed Gillie terrified, 'I *hope* you're not going to have a fever like poor Puppy; that's *just* the way his began.'

'No, no, my dear, it's nothing of that sort. I've worked rather too hard all my life, and I've got into what the doctors call a " nervous state," if you understand.'

'Nervons?' exclaimed Gillie. 'Why, what are you afraid of?'

John Ramsay felt the case to be hopeless, and hardly knew how to go on.

He made, however, one more effort.

'It is not *that* kind of nervousness, my dear child. It's a state of nervous depression, or prostration, which upsets one's digestion and prevents one sleeping at night.'

'I know!' said Gillie. 'I know exactly. I *often* have it.'

'You!' exclaimed his uncle in astonishment. 'Surely not, child?'

'Oh yes, I do!' he said: 'especially when I am sleeping in a room by myself. That's why Mrs. Pryor sleeps in my room here. I know *exactly* what you mean. So frightened that you can't get to sleep; fancying you hear odd noises, and see odd things peeping in at the hole in the shutter. Bears and wolves and things like that. It *is* horrid, isn't it? Poor Uncle John,' he added, laying his hand on

his uncle's. 'I *am* sorry you're so frightened at night.'

At this moment Mrs. Pryor appeared
in the doorway to fetch Gillie to bed.

Mr. Ramsay breathed freer when he
was gone, for he had been terribly afraid
of the conversation being continued in the
presence of the housekeeper.

His dignity did not, however, entirely
escape the blow he had been fearing would
be thus dealt to it; for as the two were
slowly ascending the big stairs, he could
hear through the door which they had left
open the child's voice evidently detailing
all that had just passed; and the concluding sentence reached him distinctly.
Mrs. Pryor was 'to be sure and give Uncle
John a night-light, as he was so frightened
all by himself in the dark.'

When Mr. Ramsay was settled in the

library, he sent for Mrs. Pryor. There were several points on which he wanted enlightenment, and he thought it probable she would be able to give him the information he required. He began by enquiring after the invalids at the Rectory. The slighter cases were doing well. The little girl with scarlatina was especially going on most favourably. Of the Rector himself it was impossible to speak with certainty.

He was no doubt very ill, and the fever running very high. The doctor felt sure it would run the full twenty-eight days.

As yet, however, there were no complications: the question was, would his strength, when the fever left him, bear the great strain put upon it?

The housekeeper's tongue was unlocked as she spoke of the Rector and his family;

and she painted in glowing colours the happy life at the Rectory; the devotion of the father to all his children, but to this child in particular, and that of the child to him. He was his father's special companion, and followed him like a little dog wherever he went.

'The little boy seems happy here,' said Mr. Ramsay. 'He seems quite at home in this place.'

The Rectory children, Mrs. Pryor explained, had always been in the habit of coming over to the Manor House to spend their half-holidays, and birthdays, etc. They had all their haunts and glory-holes, and games here. It was a little paradise to them. They could do what they liked; and there was nothing to spoil. 'They are free here, sir,' the kind woman said, 'and it's liberty that children love.'

' He seems a friendly child ? ' interrogatively.

Yes. Master Gilbert was indeed a very friendly child. He loved everybody, and everybody loved him. He had never known anything but love all his life, and he looked for it from all. It was as natural to him as the air he breathed.

How was it, Mr. Ramsay asked, that the little boy did not seem to connect any idea of danger with his father's illness, or seem at all alarmed about it?

It was Mrs. Ramsay's wish, answered Mrs. Pryor, that the child should only know what she had herself told him, namely that his father's illness must last a given time, and that he must not expect to hear he was better until that time was over.

Mrs. Ramsay understood her little boy, and knew what was best for him. She knew it was better not to overstrain him with the hope of hearing better news every day when no real change could take place for so long.

'Should any danger arise later on,' added Mrs. Pryor with a sigh, 'it would be time enough for him to be frightened.'

There was no use in saddening him and burdening his little life with a fear and a dread, which might, please God, never be realised.

'Quite so,' said Mr. Ramsay shyly. 'I can quite see the *wisdom* of the arrangement. What I wanted to know is: How is it the child himself is so easily satisfied, and so content to take other people's word for it?'

Mrs. Pryor smiled: a pitying smile for an old bachelor who understood children so little.

'Little children are always like that, sir,' she answered. 'They can't understand: they *must* trust. Master Gilbert has complete faith in everything his father or mother tell him. You see, sir, he's never known them wrong.'

She went away, and left him musing on the child's spirit: on its temper of simple, trusting faith—the spirit without which, our Lord assures us, we none of us, old or young, can enter the kingdom of Heaven.

His thoughts strayed on to other points of child-nature, of which he had had experience that day. That power of conjuring up interest and enjoyment wherever one looks, what a wonderful thing it was!

This neglected place, which to him was an eyesore, a desolation, was the very same place which, radiated by the eyes which looked upon it, was a joy and a delight.

To the clear eyes of the child on all around was the 'light which never really shone': all was bathed in ' clouds of glory.' To his own weary and worn-out eyes on all was written ' Ichabod.'

The very parts he had found so dull, so dead, were in the child's eyes, replete with fascination.

That wretched shrubbery, that dark and dirty hay-loft, that dreary kitchen-garden—were alive with his own creations.

Things, John Ramsay was beginning to discover, were as those who look upon them make them.

It is not so much the things themselves as the way you approach them.

M

The child not only created his own world, he peopled it also.

And this was not by the power of imagination. There was some other force at work here which mystified John Ramsay. The child had a power of seeing beneath appearances of which he was totally devoid.

He saw tender hearts and human feelings where he saw only 'the employed': he saw a being of hopes and fears where he saw only a stiff young footman. He did more. He penetrated beneath uninteresting and commonplace exteriors; and found there a reflection of his own love and sympathy: evoked what he bestowed. He *did* turn everything into gold, if you like, Mr. Ramsay reflected, not in the dry and prosaic way in which *he* had done; not into the cold, irresponsive metal, as did the touch at *his* fingers, but in another fashion altogether.

How the vacant expression of that soul-less-looking old clodhopper had brightened at the child's approach! How all the hidden gold of his nature had been conjured up into his face!

How much the child saw *everywhere*, to which his, John Ramsay's, eyes were closed!

'Blessed,' he said to himself half involuntarily, 'are the eyes which see the things that ye see—the ears that hear the things that ye hear—*Their* ears,' with a sudden sense of sharp contrast, 'are dull of hearing, and their eyes they have closed.'

To the seeing eye and the loving heart a brighter world rises out of the common world around.

But to blinded eyes and a hardened heart no vision is vouchsafed.

And looking at things in this light, John Ramsay reflected how much more there might be in life if he could only see it; how much more to be heard of its deep undertone, if he could only hear it! How much more in the world around him, and in those about him, than he had yet been able to discover: for

> There's a deep below the deep,
> A height above the height,
> Our hearing is not hearing,
> And our seeing is not sight.

It was a new and a far-reaching thought to one who had thought but little all his life.

His mind—to quote the expression of an American writer—was 'stretched' by it.

He pondered on it long.

.　　　.　　　.　　　.　　　.

That night, when he went to bed, Mr. Ramsay opened, with an interest he had not felt for years, the Bible his mother had given him when he went to school; and, after much searching—for he was, unhappily, out of the habit, and could not lay his finger with any ease on what he wanted—found two passages which he marked, and added the day's date.

And as he shut the book, he mused over the words of those passages; words not thought of till now for many, many years.

'Except a man be born again, he cannot see the kingdom of God,' and, 'Whosoever shall not receive the kingdom of God as a little child, he shall in no wise enter therein.'

CHAPTER IV.

A STRANGELY ASSORTED PAIR.

That which the Fountain sends forth,
Returns again to the Fountain.

THE resolution formed for the one day, seemed likely to become the ordinary rule of life ; for the next day, and the next, found this strangely assorted pair spending the best part of their time together.

John Ramsay had his reward ; for, wandering about in the lovely summer weather, hand-in-hand with his child-guide, he was daily initiated into more and more of the delights which made the old Manor House a paradise in the eyes of his little nephew.

The child saw beauty everywhere. Every nook and corner teemed with excitements. What would otherwise have seemed quite devoid of interest, became, under the teaching of the child, full of enjoyment. Everything little Gillie approached seemed to his uncle to brighten. Everything on which his young glance rested seemed to shine.

Every spot where his little presence penetrated, however uninteresting before, was radiated at once, as if the sun fell upon it.

The more John Ramsay entered into the little mind, the more he found in all around him, and the more the contrast between the child and himself forced itself upon him.

The difference between them really lay in this: The one looked through an open

glass, and saw God's world clear and
lovely; the other had put the ' quicksilver
of his own selfishness behind the glass, and
it gave him back nothing but his own
discontented face '—his own unsatisfied
and unsatisfying existence, his own failure
to make himself happy, though his life had
been spent in the effort. As if anything
that begins and ends in self could be
happy!

But he was learning something already;
learning more than he had anticipated,
when he first embarked on this strange
friendship ; learning something of the
divine lesson of self-forgetfulness, and of
all that that brings.

The third day was Sunday. It was not,
as we know, Mr. Ramsay's habit to absent
himself from church. But his brother's
church, he learnt from Mrs. Pryor, was

closed, and there was no other nearer than the county town, nine miles off. Not feeling equal to the fatigue of a long drive, he made up his mind to stay at home.

If he had supposed that such behaviour would escape comment he was soon undeceived.

Gillie entered the library early, in his Sunday best, with an unusually large-sized prayer-book under his arm, and, advancing to his uncle, asked him for a half-sheet of writing-paper. Mr. Ramsay immediately supplied him with some, and asked him, as he handed it to him, what it was for.

'I'm going to tear it into little strips to make markers, and then find my places,' answered Gillie. 'I'm rather late, and it will soon be time to be starting for church.'

'I'm not going to church,' said Mr. Ramsay, rather hesitatingly.

Gillie stopped short in the middle of the room, his prayer-book in one hand, and the sheet of writing-paper in the other. 'Not going to church?' he exclaimed.

'No, not to-day,' answered Mr. Ramsay.

'But Uncle John,' said Gillie, ' it's *Sunday*!'

' I know, my dear—I know,' and then he stopped. There was a pause and a silence, and then a rather awe-struck little voice said, ' Uncle John, are you a *heathen*?'

'No, no, my little boy! What could make you think such a thing?'

Gillie drew a long breath of relief. 'Oh ! I am so glad. You did frighten me so ; I thought, you know, perhaps, that, as you'd been so long in heathen countries, you might have got to be one, too, don't you

see? Oh! wouldn't it have been dreadful
if you had worshipped idols!'

'"Their idols are silver and gold": I'm
not quite so sure I don't,' muttered John
Ramsay to himself. 'What's the difference,
after all?'

'Uncle John,' pursued Gillie, eyeing
him curiously, 'you're not a Roman
Catholic, are you?'

'A Roman Catholic? No. Why?'

'I thought you might be, as you didn't
go to church. There was a lady staying
with us once, and she *never* came to church,
and so I asked Puppy why, and he said she
was a Roman Catholic and went to a church
of her own, only there wasn't one of hers
anywhere about here. I'm glad, though,'
he added with a sigh of relief, 'that you're
not a Roman Catholic. They're cruel
people, I think.'

'Cruel! Why?'

'They burn *insects* in church, our nursery-maid says; and I think that's very cruel, don't you? But Uncle John, as we're not going to church, I suppose you'll read prayers at home. Shall I go and ring the dinner-bell?'

'Eh! *Stop!*' called out his uncle in dismay, for Gillie had already got his hand upon the door.

'I don't think,' he said more quietly, as the little boy returned to him—'I don't think I can have any prayers.'

'Not have any prayers?'

'I'm not a clergyman you see, my dear, like your father, and I'm not accustomed to reading out loud to a lot of people. It would make me very sh——would, I mean, be a great exertion.'

'Oh, but,' said Gillie, 'it isn't Puppy

that reads prayers on wet Sundays, because of course he has to go to church whatever the weather is. It's mother, and *she's* not a clergyman, you know.'

' I'm afraid I couldn't,' said Mr. Ramsay feebly; 'I'm not in the habit you see. Reading out loud is all habit.'

He glanced nervously at the little boy to see the effect of his words.

' Oh !' said Gillie slowly, only half-satis- fied. 'Well, what shall we do then this morning ?' he went on. 'Can you think of a nice Sunday game ?'

' A nice Sunday game ?' repeated Uncle John to gain time, hoping that in the in- terval Gillie would propose something him- self to which he might assent.

'I haven't got anything here but my bricks,' Gillie said thoughtfully. 'We might build something out of the Bible you know.'

'Build something out of the Bible?' repeated Mr. Ramsay, with careful exactitude.

'Yes. Can you think of any building we hear about in the Bible?'

'The Temple?' suggested Mr. Ramsay timidly.

'*Much* too grand,' replied Gillie; 'my bricks couldn't do all those beautiful courts and things. No, it must be something easy. A tower or something like that—*I* know——' he interrupted himself joyfully, 'the tower of Babel!'

'The tower of Babel?' repeated Mr. Ramsay.

The box of bricks was fetched, and the tower rose higher and higher, under the hands of the two builders. It lasted for a great part of the morning. 'Uncle John,' said Gillie, when, after a time, they were both taking a little rest after their exertions, 'do you think it's quite right to learn French and Latin and all that?'

'Right?' answered Mr. Ramsay, puzzled, 'what could there be wrong in it?'

'Well, *I'm* not quite so sure about it,' said Gillie; 'I never feel sure if it *is* quite right.'

'But why?' exclaimed his uncle.

'Why because of that,' said Gillie, nodding toward his tower of bricks; 'I mean, don't you see, that if God wanted every one to speak different languages, it doesn't seem quite right for us to go and learn each other's, *does* it?'

Mr. Ramsay was nonplussed. He could not think what to say.

'Did you ever ask any one about it before?' he said rather nervously: 'your father or mother?'

He was anxious to share the responsibility with some one else.

'Only Jock,' answered Gillie, 'I said so to him one day.'

'Oh!' said Mr. Ramsay, rather disappointed. 'Were you building a tower of Babel together?'

'Oh no,' said Gillie, 'it was one day when he was doing a *very* difficult French exercise. He thought *just* the same as me. But he had never thought of it before, he said.'

'Ah!' said Mr. Ramsay to himself, 'Jock belongs to a certain class of nineteenth-century philosophers, in his small way.'

Gillie's conscience seemed now tho-

roughly roused. He glanced rather nervously at his tower of bricks.

'I'm not quite sure either,' he added
presently, looking rather disturbed, 'whether we *ought* to build a tower of Babel.
What do you think ? '

'Perhaps,' he continued, advancing to
the building and hastily knocking it down,
'perhaps we'd better not !'

His dinner-hour had now arrived, and
he took leave of his uncle, extorting a
promise from him, ere he went, that they
should take a 'Sunday walk' together in
the afternoon.

'Such a sad thing has happened,' he
said, running into the library about an
hour after. 'Poor old Thompson was
taken very ill this morning !'

'Who's old Thompson ?' asked Mr.
Ramsay.

N

'Oh! Uncle John. The dear old man who works in the kitchen-garden, of course.'

'Oh! I remember. I'm sorry to hear it. What is the matter with him?'

'Something very bad with his side. I forget the name.'

A pause. Gillie continued standing by his uncle in an attitude of expectancy. Mr. Ramsay having expressed his regret his sympathy (and I fear, too, his interest) was exhausted.

'Ain't you going off to see him, Uncle John?'

'Me? No, my dear! What good could I do him?'

'But, Uncle John! he's *ill*, poor man.'

'Well, my dear, *I* can't help it.'

'Puppy always goes off directly he hears any one is ill,' said Gillie, rather reproachfully; 'even if he's just sat down to dinner, he gets up directly and starts off.'

'Yes, my dear child. But I must remind you again I'm not a clergyman. Don't you see—that makes all the difference?'

'Oh! I forgot,' said Gillie.

But there was an only-half-satisfied expression on his face, which alarmed his uncle; and dreading any further misunderstandings, he tried to change the subject by proposing they should now start for the promised Sunday walk.

Gillie ran away to put on his things; and, by the time he came back, old Thompson, to Mr. Ramsay's relief, was apparently forgotten.

'What sort of man is that young footman?' asked Mr. Ramsay, as they walked along.

He had a reason for his enquiry; and he was beginning to believe in the child's insight into character.

'What—Edmund?' said Gillie. 'Oh, he's such a nice, kind man, Uncle John! I *am* so fond of him. He's always doing kind things. He'll do anything in the world for anybody.'

Mr. Ramsay was puzzled. The account did not tally with that which the butler had that morning been giving him of the person in question. He had been rather 'bothering him with complaints of the said Edmund. He had spoken of him as idle, inattentive to his work, etc.'

'Do anything for anybody?' he repeated. 'Now what kind of things?'

'Oh, well!' answered Gillie, 'he'll cut a face out of a turnip for you, if you wanted one. Or he'd bring up young blackbirds for you, or give you a ride on his back. He would, *reely*, Uncle John. And then he's not a bit *fussy*, don't you know.'

'Fussy!' repeated Uncle John. 'Now how do you mean? In what way?'

'Oh! well I mean, don't you know, that even if he's right in the middle of cleaning his plate, he'll leave it all to come and have a race with you. He'll let the bell go on ringing and ringing, if you're blowing soap-bubbles with him, or having a game of single-wicket in the yard. "*Let* them ring," he'll say. Oh! he *is* a jolly man, is Edmund. He *must* be nice and kind, mustn't he, Uncle John?'

'Oh, very!' said Mr. Ramsay, with a vivid recollection of having been kept ten minutes waiting, when he had rung the library bell, yesterday.

'Some footmen are so fussy,' proceeded

Gillie, 'they rush off directly a bell rings, and spoil games right in the middle. But Edmund's not a *bit* fussy, not one bit.'

They were now passing the gardener's cottage, and Gillie cast a longing glance at the windows.

'I wonder how poor old Thompson is by this time,' he said. 'Mr. Hobbs would be sure to know. Shall we knock at the door and ask? And oh, Uncle John, we might go in, and see Mrs. Hobbs's new baby!'

'I think—I think we won't,' said Mr. Ramsay, much alarmed. 'I don't know the gardener's wife you see, and it might—it might be very awkward.'

'Oh, but *I* do,' said Gillie. 'I know her very well indeed. She's one of my very great friends.'

'Sunday is not a good day for visiting

these kind of people,' mentioned Mr. Ramsay in desperation. 'They have their own friends, and one is rather in the way.'

It was a fortunate remark, for Gillie answered, 'Oh yes! they do. I can see through the windows several people sitting at tea. But, Uncle John, I don't think they'd think you in the way at all, for I know Mrs. Hobbs is *longing* to see you. So is Mr. Hobbs, and lots of the people round about. They say it seems so strange to have a master they do not know, and have never seen—— Shall I tell you a secret, Uncle John? Mrs. Hobbs is going to ask you to be godfather to the new baby!'

He paused for a moment to view the effect on his uncle of the announcement of the impending honour.

'Eh!' said John Ramsay aghast; but Gillie took the expression for one of gratified surprise.

'Yes!' he said delighted, 'it's quite true, *reely*! The only thing she's not quite sure about is whether you'd like it called " Ramsay " or " John." Which do you think sounds best with " Hobbs "?'

Before the godfather-elect could express an opinion, Gillie went on—

'You'll kiss the baby at the christening, won't you, Uncle John? Because Mrs. Hobbs says she would rather you had the first kiss after it's christened than anybody in the world. She remembers hearing her father talk about *your* christening, she says; and he knew your father, and your grandfather, you see.'

Mr. Ramsay muttered something inaudible. He was beginning to realise with a pang that 'property has its duties as well as its rights.' Gillie, however, was quite content to take cordial assent for granted, and they walked on. After the gardener's cottage had been safely left behind Gillie started a new subject.

'Why do you always say "the footman" and "the housekeeper" and "the gardener"?' he asked.

'Why, what else should I say?' asked Mr. Ramsay.

'Why, "Edmund" and "Mrs. Pryor" and "Mr. Hobbs," of course,' said Gillie. 'Is it that you can't remember their names? Is that why?'

Mr. Ramsay was silent. He was conscious that herein lay one of those differences between him and the child on which he had been dwelling a few nights before;

that where he saw only machines necessary for his comfort and well-being, little Gillie saw individuality and human fellowship.

He began quite to dread what the child would say next. But there was a deeper thrust coming. 'Uncle John,' the little fellow said, as they neared the house at the conclusion of their walk, 'I never knew till to-day that it was *only* clergymen who were kind to poor people.'

Three times Mr. Ramsay began to speak, and three times he stopped abruptly. He tried to form a sentence each time by which to excuse, if not to exculpate, himself; but none of them seemed to him to express at all what he wanted to say. He gave it up altogether at last, for everything he attempted appeared to him to partake

of the nature of the familiar French pro-
verb—*Qui s'excuse s'accuse.*

He thought perhaps actions would be
more convincing than words. He put his
hand into his pocket.

'Look here, Gillie,' he said, taking a
couple of half-crowns out, and handing
them to the little boy, ' you may send the
footm——I mean Edmund—with these to
old Thompson, and say they are a present
from me. Then he can buy whatever is
necessary, either of food or medicine.'

' Oh, Uncle John! Uncle John!' exclaimed the child in delight. '*How* pleased
he will be! Five shillings—why I don't
suppose he's *ever* in his life had so much
money all at once before! But *why* should
we send Edmund with it? *Do* let us take
it to him ourselves. I should so like to see
his joy. And I'm sure if you came and

gave it to him *yourself*, he would be much more pleased with it. He would think a great deal more of it. He would, *reely*, Uncle John!'

He stood, looking eagerly up into his uncle's face, the unconscious exponent of Lowell's beautiful thought—

> Not what we give, but what we share,
> For the gift without the giver is bare.

But there was no answer to his appeal; and something in the face he was looking at must have chilled him, for he said nothing more. He went away to his tea, and Mr. Ramsay returned to the library, without the matter being cleared up between them.

But the latter was uneasy and perturbed. He was provoked with himself for not having thought of some tangible excuse, which might have satisfied the

child. He kept on telling himself he
'might have said this,' or he 'might have
said that.'

He had plenty of time to think it all
over, for it was a long while before Gillie
came back to him. When he appeared
Mr. Ramsay nervously fancied the child
looked grave and thoughtful.

'What are you thinking about?' he
asked anxiously. He rather courted an
opportunity of righting himself in the
child's eyes, and was now prepared to
offer to go with him to old Thompson,
if no middle course presented itself.

But he was too late. He had missed
his opportunity, one of those golden ones
which come across people's paths every
now and then, and, if missed, perhaps
never re-occur.

'I was thinking of old Thompson,'

answered the little boy, 'he *is* so bad, poor old man!'

'Have you seen him?' asked Mr. Ramsay, rather crestfallen.

'Yes. Mrs. Pryor took me after tea. And we gave him the five shillings.'

'And was he as pleased as you expected?'

'Oh! he was so pleased,' said Gillie; 'so pleased that he took both my hand and kissed them! But he said some funny things I didn't quite understand, but Mrs. Pryor said she knew what he meant. I asked her about it coming home, but it seemed to make her feel inclined to cry, and she gave me a great many kisses. Wasn't it funny?'

'What sort of things did he say?' asked Mr. Ramsay.

'Oh! I don't know. Something about

a loving heart being worth all the money in the world, and about a " bright face " and a " bit of sunshine." I didn't understand what he meant.'

But Mr. Ramsay was like Mrs. Pryor : he did.

' Do you know, Uncle John,' said Gillie, ' that we haven't read anything in the Bible, or had any prayers all day long, though it is Sunday ? I haven't even said a hymn or a text. Don't you think we'd better read a chapter together before I go to bed ? '

It was quite impossible for Mr. Ramsay to refuse any more requests of the child's to-night. He was only too glad of an opportunity of retrieving his character. Gillie fetched a Bible and suggested that they should ' look over each other ' and read verse and verse about. He was afraid he read *rather* slow, and the long words he sometimes made mistakes with, but Uncle John must not mind.

No; Uncle John promised not to mind.

It then became a question of what chapter should be chosen. Mr. Ramsay kept very quiet, hoping every minute Gillie would make his own selection.

'Look here, Uncle John,' said Gillie, looking up with a beaming smile, '*you* may choose. Tell me one of your favourite chapters, and then we will read that.'

Mr. Ramsay's face grew rather troubled. His brow contracted with anxious thought.

But he was determined not to fail again. He *must* keep up his character if possible.

Happily for him, his memory had been refreshed by the search of the night before after those passages he had marked ; and he timidly suggested the 18th Chapter of St. Matthew ; it being the only one he could recall at the moment.

Gillie was delighted. It was one of his mother's favourite chapters, too : especially all the first part.

Wasn't it funny that she and Uncle John should both happen to be so very fond of the same chapter ?

So verse by verse they read the lesson, and then Gillie kissed his uncle, and went to bed, leaving John Ramsay musing over what they had been reading, and wondering how much of it Gillie had understood—how much his little mind had taken in.

It seemed to him impossible that a child could in any way adapt to its own

O

comprehension, the deep truths of the Bible.

Yet how earnestly he had listened; how attentively he had read.

How much did he understand of it? What did it convey to him?

John Ramsay had not realised that the Word of God is capable of infinite expansion, and of infinite compression. So that what fits a child in its way, and as far as he is able at the time to understand it, fits him also as he advances in knowledge and experience; taking ever deeper meanings as life goes on.

It says one thing to us at seven, another at seventeen, and another at forty; in the same words conveying the ever-unfolding message; in the same words teaching the young, the old, the ignorant, and the wise : another testimony, if any were wanted, to the 'endless vigour and vitality of the words of Holy Scripture.'

From that his thoughts wandered on to the depth and earnestness of a child's conscience. He was as much struck by it this evening, as he had been a few nights before by the implicitness and simplicity of a child's faith.

Then he reflected on the kindness of the little heart, its tenderness and sympathy, its consideration for the feelings and well-being of others—its desire to share its happiness with all.

The child seemed to him the embodiment of Faith and Charity.

Old Thompson, too, played a part in his meditations.

Thoughts, fanciful enough for a pro·

saic man, passed over the stage of his fancy.
Dreamy ideas of how, if the old man were
called away that night ; the sunny, guileless
face at his bedside would have spoken to
him of the angels he was soon to see!

CHAPTER V.

AT HIS CHILD-TEACHER'S FEET.

Who gives himself with his alms feeds three:
Himself, his hungering neighbour, and Me.

AND so it came to pass that, as the days
went on, Mr. Ramsay grew more and more
dependent on the child's companionship.

By the end of a week or so he could
not bear to be without him even for an
hour; and if the sunny presence was not
with him, he felt everything to be uninteresting, and as if the light had gone out
of his day. He became less and less willing, too, to share him with others.

He was disappointed if he stayed away

with Mrs. Pryor, or Edmund, or any of his numerous friends.

'It is quite natural,' he would say to himself again as he sat listening to the merry voice in the court-yard sometimes, 'the footman is young, and I am——'

Here he would sigh, for he really thought it very disagreeable. He would wait and listen to every sound, and prick up his ear when the light hurrying footstep was heard, and look up eagerly for the first sight of the bright face, with a glad 'Here you are, my little boy!'

His mind and attention were now entirely concentrated on the child, and on the life they were living together.

It was quite in the spirit of children that he was living. The present was all.

He did not look forward and wonder what was to happen when the three weeks

were over; he only lived from day to
day.

The original resolution formed for self-
pleasing, and then in the desire not to
disappoint the ideal the child had formed
of him, had been followed by a feeling
which he, perhaps, could not have defined ;
but which, if put into words, might have
been construed into a wish in some mea-
sure to atone for the blight he had been the
means of bringing upon his home, and for
the fact that the only shadow which lay
upon his sunny path was of his creating.

But even this motive was now passing
into the desire to win his affection, to
make and to keep him happy, to be the
means of bringing the sparkle of joy into
the innocent eyes, the quick flush of pleasure into the little face.

It was becoming by degrees his main

thought to please one so intensely capable of pleasure, to provide enjoyment where it gave such great, such infinite, gratification.

Dawning upon him was the wish to provide the pleasure instead of to partake of it; and, in accordance with the law of action and reaction, the reflex joy was enough for him, and his own share fell into the background.

He sighed no more for his own power of enjoyment, vanished so long ago!

He was entering daily into the meaning of the axiom that 'to love is to go out of self'; becoming daily convinced that you must give if you hope to receive.

He was learning it practically as well as theoretically.

For, to begin with, in order to keep the child with him—haunted as he ever was

by the fear of his finding him a dull companion and leaving him—he worked hard
to please him.

Any one who knows anything about
children, will understand that all this involved a good deal of self-sacrifice, and
could only be done at some personal cost;
that often he must have to do things he
would rather not do, often exert himself
when he would rather rest.

He was determined not only to win
but to retain the child's friendship; and
with this end in view, he, without hardly
knowing it, sank self more and more, and
lived almost entirely in another.

With such constant study, and companionship, he grew, of course, pretty well
versed in children's ways; but he con-
tinned, nevertheless, to have many surprises. Their peculiarities were a continual

puzzle to him.   Such things, among others,
as the frequent 'It is so nasty, *do* taste
it,' 'It smells so horrid, *do* come and smell
it,' caused him much astonishment, before
he grew familiar with them.

'What a very curious thing!' he reflected in his matter-of-fact way.   'Now, if
it had been anything *nice*, one could have
understood it.'

Then the power of drawing amusement
from trifles and from common little mistakes incident to daily life puzzled him
very much.

He could not conceive why any little
foolish thing he did or said in a fit of
absence of mind, should afford Gillie such
intense enjoyment.

'What is that funny little song I so
often hear you singing'—he asked one
day—'something about a wasp and a fly?'

The child burst into a merry laugh.
'Not a *wasp*, Uncle John—a *bee*, a humble
bee.'

'Well, it's a funny little song, whatever
the insect may be. Sing it again, will you?'

He was thinking how it had sounded
outside the library window, before he had
known how dear the little singer was going
to be to him.

'Will you sing it with me?' said Gillie
eagerly. 'I'll sing the first part, and you
join in the chorus.'

Which they accordingly did; drumming their fists upon the table by way of
accompaniment.

Gillie was delighted with the perform-
ance, and with his uncle's voice.

'You sing beautifully, Uncle John,' he
said, 'we'll often sing together now. But
remember,' he added, going off again into

fits of merry laughter, 'it isn't a wasp, it's a bee. You *do* make funny mistakes, don't you? Do you remember how you poured milk instead of water into the teapot at breakfast this morning?'

The mistake was one of those to which we referred just now, and it had at the time caused Gillie such infinite amusement that Mr. Ramsay had reflected then, as he did now, what a fund was in store for him, if such little mistakes of common occurrence were able to contribute so largely to it.

Taking salt instead of sugar, helping yourself twice to salt, etc., why, the dullest life, he reflected, would afford these little incidents.

After all, how many old jokes of this kind there are in the world—poor to begin with, and now well-nigh worn out by constant use!

People must so often have said ten
stone instead of ten pounds; or twelve feet
instead of twelve inches; and yet how
inevitable the amusement such mistakes
call forth.

But it was not only in these ways, but
from trifles of all kinds, that Gillie drew
amusement and pleasure.

There seemed to Mr. Ramsay no limit
to his power of enjoyment, to his zest and
freshness in every pursuit; to the joys and
interests that sprang up in his daily path.

He had, however, one day another
experience of children's natures in this
respect: and learned that, though trifles
give them pleasure, in the same proportion trifles bring them trouble too.

As he stood shaving in the early
morning near the open window of his bedroom, he heard low sobbing in the garden

below. 'Oh dear! oh dear!' sounded in the little voice he loved so dearly, 'what *shall* I do? what *shall* I do? I shall never be happy again!'

Lightning is the only word to express the speed with which Mr. Ramsay completed his toilette, and was down in the garden; searching for the little boy, in order to discover—and, if it lay in his power, to remove—the cause of his grief.

Gillie had, however, disappeared, and he could see no trace of him anywhere.

He searched, he called, but in vain.

'Have you seen the child?' he asked eagerly of the gardener, as he passed him at his work.

'Master Gilbert is in the shrubbery, I think, sir,' was the answer, and Mr. Ramsay sped hastily on.

But long before he reached the shrubbery, Gillie came running to meet him, no
trace of tears in his eyes; no signs of grief
in his countenance.

'What is it, Uncle John?' he said.
'Did I hear you calling me?'

'Yes, my little fellow. What *was* the
matter? What *were* you crying so bitterly
about just now?'

The child looked puzzled. 'Crying?'
he repeated. 'I forget--oh yes, I know!--
I had lost something' (looking rather
shame-faced), 'and I couldn't find it *anywhere*. I hunted and hunted and *couldn't*
find it. But I found it at last,' he added,
all the joyous animation returning to his
manner, 'and I *am* so glad. I wouldn't
have lost it for all the world.'

'What was it you had lost?' enquired
his uncle, wondering what possession could

be so valuable as to be worthy of such grief at its loss.

'Oh, Uncle John, it was that *darling, darling* little pill-box you gave me—oh, wouldn't it have been dreadful if I had lost it? But you see I've found it again now. Here it is. So it's all right,' and he ran back into the shrubbery, leaving his uncle greatly wondering.

He had never seen him before in one of those sudden fits of almost causeless despair, to which all keenly enjoying, quick-feeling children are liable.

And it brought into his mind, for the first time, a doubt whether, after all, childhood *is* such a happy time as older people are apt to consider it; and whether to feel little troubles and disappointments so keenly is not in itself an insuperable bar to the joy of childhood of which these older

people talk so much.   After all, is the advantage all on their side, if trifles have such a
power to make them unhappy?

Those far on in life's journey, with their
maturer knowledge of its trials and disappointments, are perhaps too apt to look
upon children's trivial troubles as out of
all proportion to the grief and tears they
waste upon them.

But though they look infinitesimal from
our point of view, they are very real, for
the moment, from theirs.

They are really quite in proportion.
Take, for instance, the case of a baby who
can only just walk, and consider if we
shall ever know a keener disappointment
than that suffered by such a being, who,
having with intense difficulty risen to its
feet, and with still greater difficulty toddled
across the room to get hold of something

P

on a distant table, on which its heart is set, to see the hand of authority remove the prize beyond its reach.

No wonder the small baffled being sinks down upon the ground in an agony of fury and disappointment. Sometimes though, as we have seen, Gillie had real and more lasting phases of sadness, and would sit very quiet, without speaking for a long while.

When at such times lovingly questioned by his uncle it would come out that he was ' thinking of poor Puppy, and wishing he had not got to be so ill for such a long time.'

These fits. of sadness Mr. Ramsay had learned to dread. He could not bear to see the bright face clouded.

He dreaded to see the shade of thoughtfulness coming over the face which he knew would culminate in the attack of home-sickness and depression; and he would do almost anything in the world to avert it.

If the cloud were there, he would work hard to chase it away, and to bring the sunshine back.

All this gradual merging of self in the child was teaching John Ramsay much.

And besides, it could not stop at Gillie himself. To be in sympathy with so widely loving and tender-hearted a being, he was obliged perforce to extend, or at any rate to affect to extend, his interest to others.

His human sympathies began to awake within him, and to flow forth to those around.

Not spontaneously exactly, but vicariously, as it were, through, and for the sake of, the child.

It was for love of him, and to keep up his character in his eyes, that he began to do acts of kindness to his poorer neighbours.

That is, he gave money to Gillie to distribute.

He had no idea of charity as yet but to put his hand into his pocket, though that in itself was a great advance in a man of his habits and disposition.

He delighted in giving Gillie larger sums than he either expected or wished for : partly that he might have the pleasure of seeing his joy and surprise ; and partly because he liked the little boy to think him generous and munificent.

His own idea of the poor, as a class, was of grasping people, who wished to get all they could out of the rich ; simply and solely from love of money, and of what money brought.

He often smiled to himself when he saw Gillie picking nosegays of flowers, or filling baskets with strawberries to take to some of his friends. 'Dear simple little fellow,' he would say to himself, 'what do *those* sort of people care for that?'

But when he began (unwillingly enough) to accompany him in his visits; and, sitting stiff and silent in a corner, watched Gillie distributing his bounties, his eyes opened to a new truth in the matter of giving. He began to see why all that the child did for others was crowned with success; why his own little gifts were doubly welcome; and why his sunny presence enhanced the value of all that he brought.

Who gives *himself* with his alms . . .

Ah! that was little Gillie's secret, as it is
the secret of all true almsgiving.

> That is no gift which the hand can hold:
> He gives nothing but worthless gold
>   Who gives from a sense of duty.
> But he who gives a slender mite,
> And gives to that which is out of sight—
>   That thread of the all-sustaining beauty
> Which runs through all, and doth all unite—
> The hand cannot clasp the whole of his alms,
> The heart outstretches its eager palms:
> *For a god goes with it, and makes it store*
> *To a soul that was starving in darkness before.*

CHAPTER VI.

CHANGED VIEWS.

And the lawyers smiled that afternoon
As he hummed in court an old love tune.

A⊤ the end of a fortnight Mr. Ramsay received a letter from his old clerk in London, urging him to come up, if only for the day, to transact some business.

Strange to say the idea gave him no pleasure.

On the contrary, the feeling uppermost in his mind on reading the letter was one bordering on annoyance.

He had lost all wish for what, a fortnight before, he had so longed and sighed for.

His views on the subject had undergone a change.

He felt now that it would be a sad waste of a June day, to spend it in the city of London; and he felt even more strongly that to spend a whole day away from Gillie would be thoroughly distasteful to him.

However, he had no valid excuse to offer. He was so much stronger in mind and body that he knew he was quite equal to the exertion; and he knew, too, that there must be, by this time, an accumulation of business to which he ought to attend.

He telegraphed back to say he would be in London the next morning, and then nothing remained but to announce his intentions to Gillie.

'Oh, Uncle John!' exclaimed the little

fellow in dismay, '*please* don't go away.   I can't let you.   What *should* I do without you?'

Mr. Ramsay's intention wavered still more.

Gillie never knew how nearly he gave it all up, and let dividends and investments take their chance.

When the next morning came he felt quite depressed at the idea of parting with the child, and a lump came into his throat as he wished him good-bye.   It was curious how depressing he thought London that day, how dark and how dull he felt the city to be.   The sight of his old clerk brought back only wearisome associations.

He found his thoughts, as he sat at work in his business-room, constantly turning to the lovely country and the bright summer sights and sounds he had left behind him, continually wandering to the little central figure which illumined it all, wondering what the child was doing —whether he missed him, or whether he was quite happy without him—following with his mental eye all the occupations of his little day, saying, almost out loud, 'Now he's working in his garden. Now he's feeding his birds. . . .'

What a dingy hole this London lodging was! How dark! How oppressive! How dismal!

What a noise and din in the streets outside! What an incessant roll and roar in one's ears instead of that deep stillness of the country, broken only by the song of the birds—by the laugh of the woodpecker —Is he listening to it now? . . .

He *must* stop this day-dreaming, and go on with his business.

But the thought of the child pursued him still.

He could almost see him skipping about on the terrace: almost hear his light dancing footsteps, and gay voice, singing his quaint little song.

Mr. Ramsay's old clerk came once or twice to the door of his business-room that day, to ask if he had called: for most unusual sounds had proceeded from within.

But no! Mr. Ramsay had not called.

He was sitting, writing, as usual: and seemed surprised at the interruption.

The third time the clerk did not like to open the door and disturb his master with the same enquiry; and yet he felt almost sure this time that he had called out. So he paused for a moment outside, and became aware, to his astonishment, that his

master was *humming*. Humming and—
singing!

But silence followed, and the scratching
of the busy pen. Relieved by that accustomed sound, the clerk was retiring, when
a fresh outburst startled and arrested him.

With renewed vigour the singing began
again, and this time the words were louder,
and quite distinct—

> Says the Fly, says she,
> 'Will you marry me,
> And live with me,
> Sweet humble Bee?'

The clerk's face assumed a rather grave
aspect, and he slightly shook his head.

He looked cautiously all round him,
especially towards the room he had just
left, as if hoping no one but himself was
within earshot. All was now quite quiet
again inside his master's room, and the
scratching of the pen again audible.

Suddenly, louder than ever, and accompanied by stamping of feet, and what sounded like the drumming of fists upon the table, it broke out again.

> Fiddle-de-dee !
> Fiddle-de-dee !
> The Fly has married the humble Bee.

The old clerk's face grew very long indeed, and his eyes round and scared-looking. He retired very, very quietly, shutting every door behind him, and shaking his head sorrowfully. For he was loyal and true; and in his way loved the silent, abstracted man he had served so long.

He had been distressed enough already at the breakdown in his nerves and brain-power; but he had not expected anything so bad as this! In all these many years he had never heard him hum or sing before. And as to drumming with his fists!—and stamping!—and in the middle of business, too! 'Ah! well, it was very sad, *very* sad—but the less said about it the better!'

A few hours later the object of these gloomy forebodings was tearing along in the train on his way home, enjoying the, to him, novel sensation that some one was waiting for him, and expecting him and longing for his return.

He felt quite excited when he got into the carriage waiting at the station and drove off towards home.

He strained his eyes as he neared the lodge-gate, in hopes of catching sight of a little figure, on its way to meet him.

Yes; there it was! There was the little fellow holding the gate open and waving his hat.

The carriage was stopped, and Mr. Ramsay got eagerly out, Gillie springing into his arms, with a welcome as fervent as if they had been parted for years : his bright face belying his assurances that he had been ' so dreadfully dull without him.'

Hand in hand, the reunited friends walked home through the chestnut avenue, Mr. Ramsay feeling—as he drank in the beauty of the summer evening, and listened to Gillie's merry prattle of all that he had done during his absence—that he could never go away again.

How calm and fresh the country seemed after the long hot day in the city ! How sweet the smell of the new-mown hay and the roses !

He woke next morning with a feeling of intense relief, that his visit to London lay behind him, and that this day, and the

next, and the next, could be devoted to
Gillie once more.

How pleasant it was to sit in the library
after breakfast, with that delicious sense of
leisure and repose ! listening to the child's
gay laugh upon the terrace, while the
scent of the limes floated in at the
window.

He leant back in his chair with a
feeling of calm satisfaction that he was
once again free to be the sharer in childish
avocations and simple pleasures, that his
day was once more in the little boy's
hands, and that he had only to follow in
his lead.

The days were so precious, too : for
the time was drawing on when the " three
weeks " of little Gillie's calculations would
be over.   Already a fortnight was gone.

Beyond those three weeks John Ramsay

did not allow himself to look. He knew they must come to an end, that the termination of his brother's illness, either way, must result in the child being taken from him, but he turned his thoughts resolutely away from the future. He had got into a little oasis in the desert of his life, and he would not allow himself to think of the waste that probably lay beyond.

For the time, the child was all his own. . . .

'I am going to the dogs,' said a gay voice; and a bright, innocent face, which seemed out of harmony with the announcement, peeped in at the window. 'Will you come, too?'

Mr. Ramsay immediately rose from his chair and took his way to the terrace. Conversation flowed freely as the two

Q

walked along towards the kennels; and they had nearly reached their destination when Gillie suddenly stopped short, and gave an exclamation of dismay.

'What is it?' said Mr. Ramsay.

'My letter to mother,' he said; 'I quite forgot to finish it before I came out. I must go back.'

'We'll go back together,' said Mr. Ramsay.

'I don't like to disappoint the poor dogs,' said Gillie; 'Uncle John, won't you go on and feed them, and I'll come back to you as fast as I can after I've finished my letter?'

Of course Mr. Ramsay would do anything that Gillie asked him: and he waited patiently while the child transferred from his own pocket to his uncle's every sort of horrible old bone, which he had been saving up from the breakfast and dinner plates.

'I sha'n't be long' he said, when this operation was over. 'I've only got to write the good-byes and the P.C.'

'The P.C.?' repeated Mr. Ramsay; 'what's that?'

'The thing at the end of a letter, you know,' explained Gillie.

'Oh—the postscript! Do you always think it necessary to put a postscript to your letters?'

'Oh, yes, of course!' he answered, 'every letter has to have a P.C. It wouldn't be a letter, not a proper one at least, without. But I shall be very quick, Uncle John. I shall run after you as fast as possible.'

Mr. Ramsay strolled on, and fulfilled his mission.

Q 2

Gillie was a long time coming, but as letter-writing was always a difficult process with him, his uncle was not surprised at his non-appearance.

The P.C. was evidently a more lengthy affair than he had anticipated.

Mr. Ramsay returned to the house, in hopes of meeting him, but missed him somehow on the way, and on reaching the library found it empty.

The letter, however, lay finished on the blotting-book, ready to be folded up, and put into its envelope—a task which always fell to Mr. Ramsay's share.

He advanced to the writing-table, to take it up, and stood aghast at the sight of the startling piece of intelligence which was about to find its way into the quiet country rectory.

'P.C.—Uncle John has gone to the

dogs, and I am going after him as fast as possible.'

They had been talking together a day or two before Mr. Ramsay went to London about keeping diaries, and Mr. Ramsay had expatiated on their great interest as you get on in life, and your memory begins to fail.

He regretted, he had said, that he had not kept one all his life.

Gillie had been fired to begin at once.

'Uncle John, *do, do* give me a book to keep it in, and let me begin directly.'

' You, my little fellow? I am afraid you would never have the perseverance to go on every day.'

'But when I am *determined*, Uncle John, when I make up my mind, I *reely* should.'

Accordingly a diary had been procured

by Mr. Ramsay in London, and Gillie was
now presented with it.

There was a good many sighs and
groans over it that evening in the library
as he wrote in the distance, perched up at
Mr. Ramsay's own business-table, with an
enormous inkstand in front of him.

Looking round at him presently as a
very deep sigh escaped him, Mr. Ramsay
saw him in an attitude of deep thought,
with a large quill pen stuck behind his ear.

'What is the matter, Gillie?'

'Oh, Uncle John, how *do* you spell
" determined "? It *is* such a long word.'

Letter by letter Uncle John patiently
dictated it.

'There!' said Gillie in a tone of
triumph ; 'now it's done, and now I shall
write a little bit of it *every day* of my life,
all my life long.'

'Let me see what you have done,' said Mr. Ramsay.

Gillie scrambled down from his high elevation, and handed the journal to his uncle.

Mr. Ramsay took it in his hands, and found in large text-hand the following entry—

June 22.—' Determined to keep a Dairy.'

Years after he found that journal in an old cupboard. But—alas for the futility of human resolutions—it was the only entry in the book.

CHAPTER VII.

THE CHURCH IN THE OLD COUNTY-TOWN.

Thou blessed child,
There was a time when pure as thou,
I looked and prayed like thee—but now!—MOORE.

THE Sunday after that no excuses were made for not going to church.

John Ramsay felt a wish to go there with his child-companion.

He felt quite up to the long drive to the county-town; more especially when he found what a pleasure nine miles in a dog-cart would be to Gillie.

At about ten o'clock that small person presented himself in the library, as on the former occasion, with his large prayer-book under his arm, and a request for a sheet of notepaper.

'We shall just have time,' he said, 'to find my places.'

His prayer-book, with his uncle's assistance, was soon bristling with white paper marks in every direction.

He heaved a deep sigh as he laid it on the table.

'Now,' he said, 'I shall be all right, and you won't have to keep whispering to me, "Psalms," "Litany," "Collect," and all that.'

Nothing certainly could have been further from Mr. Ramsay's intentions, but he was always glad to get a hint of what might be expected from him under new circumstances.

The drive was in every way delightful,

and they arrived at the church door just as the bell had ceased ringing.

It was a large, crowded church, for the town was a considerable one; and it was a few minutes before seats were found for them at the far end of a pew already fairly well filled. Gillie had some difficulty in steering himself and his large prayer-book, with its quills sticking out in every direction, safely across the knees and feet of all the people over whom he had to pass on his way.

Mr. Ramsay followed him as best he could; and, after seating himself, was bending slightly over the hollow of his hand to say a few words of prayer, when the look of blank astonishment in the innocent eyes of the child at his side made him feel rebuked, and caused him to bethink himself and to assume a more reverent attitude.

The service presently began, and all went well until after the reading of the first lesson.

And now a terrible disaster occurred.

In rising from his seat at the 'Te Deum' Gillie either opened his prayer-book too hastily or stood up too suddenly.

But be that as it may his prayer-book received a shake and half dropped from his hand.

The result was that a perfect snow-storm of little white papers fell fluttering in every direction; and an exclamation of dismay burst from their distracted owner.

'Oh, my marks, my marks!' escaped his lips in an awestruck whisper, while a scared and agonised expression overspread his whole countenance.

The big prayer-book was now a trackless desert, through which, unaided, he would never find his way.

All landmarks were gone for ever. Signposts, mile-stones—all had disappeared.

He put the book down on the seat beside him in mute despair, and an ominous silence followed.

Presently, something like the sound of a sob made Mr. Ramsay start.

He looked quickly round. Quiet tears were falling, and suppressed ejaculations of sorrow were plainly to be heard.

'Oh, what shall I do? What shall I do? It's no use now. I shall never, never be able to find any of my places again.'

He stood disconsolate, the ground beneath him strewn with the wrecks of his former hopes.

Much alarmed, Uncle John bent over

him, whispering words of consolation, but feeling very uncertain of his powers.

The reading of the second lesson gave him an opportunity of sitting down and drawing the child towards him.

By the time it was over, Gillie had re-covered himself, and a whispered com-pact had been made between him and his uncle that they should share a prayer-book together for the rest of the service.

Mr. Ramsay got very nervous, as the service proceeded, when he perceived Gillie's searching and enquiring gaze fixed upon certain little columns of figures which appeared every now and then on the margin of the leaves, and which he had fondly hoped the child would not observe. They were figures, as we know, which he would very much rather not be questioned about. He was glad when, the last hymn being over, he was able to put his prayer-book into his pocket ; and hoped that even if observed they might be forgotten by the time the sermon was over.

Gillie nestled up to his uncle and rested his head on his shoulder. The dear little hand slipped itself confidingly into his. Its contact sent a strange thrill to John Ramsay's heart.

The sermon began.

It is a curious thing to look at a congregation of people hanging on the words of one man : their minds and intellects held, as it were, in the grasp of another, and turned and swayed at his will—impregnated for the moment with his spirit, imbued with his' thoughts and feelings. Expanding under his influence, as he warms with his subject, they judge as he judges, deduce as he deduces, and rise with him into that higher atmosphere, from whence all here below is more justly judged of and balanced.

There is a very special way of looking on things in church—a 'changed view of all vital matters.'

The quiet and leisure to *think* even, comes to some only there.

Their outlook on life is changed for the moment, and people dimly realise that there *is* something more important than their daily interests and occupations; something that transcends even worldly advancement or the making of money; something that will last when all these things have passed away.

It may fade, and *will* fade when they get out of church, and be lost in the interests which will meet them outside the door; but for the time they are under its influence.

The power of the Unseen is upon them, and they have a sense that the present, the visible, the tangible, is slipping, slipping from them, and that they *must* one day let it go. That they are dreaming in a land of mists and shadows which obscure for a moment the reality and the substance beyond.

'A preacher,' says Gordon, 'stands before his congregation as a man before a garden full of seeds, which he has to water in order to vivify with life. He is the channel of communication. If the man is worldly minded, the channel of communication is clogged, and his preaching will be feeble.'

But the man to whom John Ramsay was listening was not worldly minded, and he was, therefore, a powerful channel of communication to his hearers.

'So soon,' is the text he has chosen, 'so soon passeth it away, and we are gone.' He is putting life before them as a whole; spreading it out before them as a field wherein great things may be done; and forcing upon them the conviction that each one of them can and may do them; is, in short, the man or woman who alone can do them in his or her own small sphere; in the little niche of God's world allotted to them.

Life as a whole; not the little bit by which they are at the moment surrounded; in which they are for time engrossed; but the whole field of life, past, present, and to come, with the one golden purpose running through.

He gathers in one, as it were, all the tangled threads of each man's varying life

R

and circumstances, and presents it to his mental vision as one whole—an intricate pattern indeed, but one out of which a beautiful thing may be made.

A strong conviction of your own brings conviction to others.

What he seems to see so clearly, they too begin to see.

He has raised the minds and hearts of his hearers to a high level, and now he is able to force them to see life from that point of view.

His words are forcible in themselves, but it is the sense of his own conviction behind them which carries them so straight home to his hearers.

He has embued them with his own earnestness, his own enthusiasm, his own high aims and lofty aspirations. He has raised all life to a higher platform by the way he views it himself, by his deep sense of its great aim and end, and he has raised each man's life in his **own** eyes to a higher possibility by the capabilities he has shown it to contain.

For the moment all things seem possible, and each hearer's better self rises up with the heartfelt cry, ' Behold *I* come, to do Thy will, oh Lord!'

In the garden of seeds before which he was standing there were, doubtless, many that day in whom life was watered and vivified, but we are concerned only with one.

John Ramsay had not listened long before a new feeling for which he could not account came gradually stealing over him. He experienced the sense of being held in the moral grasp of another. **He** found himself, he hardly knew how, being lifted up out of the slough of his usual worldly ways of thinking and judging.

Different ideas of failure and of success, new views of the meanings of those words, came floating down upon him.

He felt he was looking at life *at last* from the right point of view, the view which a hundred years hence every soul in that congregation would feel to be the right, the only, point of view. And seen in this light, the success of his worldly, successful life looked like failure, and his own failure to find happiness in it looked like the first gleam of success.

Every word hit like a hammer; every shot went home; and brought before him so clear a conviction of his wasted existence— the aimless, purposeless years lying behind him; the total absence of a golden thread of holy purpose running through—as to be almost pain.

The dormant nature of his spiritual part all this time came before him with a sharp pang. Dormant! Not only dormant, but non-existent—dead.

Not only dead, but buried. Every avenue to his spirit choked, stopped up by the love of money, and the absorbing interest arising therefrom which had possessed him for forty years, to the exclusion, the inevitable exclusion, of every better or higher thought; every interest, every aspiration.

A man without a soul, a 'spiritual giant buried under a mountain of gold,' in whom riches had, indeed, 'choked the word,' and from whom God and everlasting truth were shut out. It must ever be so when every thought is fixed upon an earthly end or object. It need not be money, of course. It may be cares, it may be pleasure, it may be worldly ambition, it may even be an engrossing pursuit, or an absorbing human affection.

But whatever it be the result is the same.

The kingdom of God, the power of the Unseen, is shut out. It cannot enter. How *can* it when every avenue is closed ?

As well might you expect the fresh air to enter a room which for disinfecting purposes has had its doors and windows pasted up, and its fireplace hermetically sealed.

'The kingdom of Heaven,' says our Lord, 'is *within* you '—but into such no entrance can it find.

A seed had been planted in the dried-up soil of John Ramsay's heart by the contemplation of the guileless child-life he had had during the past fortnight before him; and now it is being watered and vivified.

The better life is beginning to waken, the higher nature beginning to stir.

It is rising from its long grave. Gazing down upon the innocent little face cradled on his arm he again thought of the stainless innocence of that little life, and of the contrast it offered to his own.

The child seemed to him the embodiment of the atmosphere around him; the tangible shape of his own vague imaginations; and the living representation of his new thoughts.

He thought how different life must appear to the mental vision of such a guileless spirit; looking out upon life with its clear gaze, and colouring everything with its own purity.

He found himself shrinking from the thought of a day ever coming, when the child should learn to be like him: 'the covetous man who is an idolater,' of whom it is expressly said that he has *no* inheritance in the kingdom of Christ and of God.

And yet *once*, he bitterly thought, *once* his outlook had been as innocent, as pure.

A feeling of passionate regret for his past innocence came over him.

Why had he not died in his childhood?

Then a feeling of dread for Gillie's future.

Why could he not always remain as pure and innocent as he was now?

Better for him, John Ramsay, far better, had he been taken away with his young mother, and laid to rest for ever by her side.

Better, a thousand times better, for Gillie to be translated now, in his innocent state, to the kingdom where such pure young spirits dwell.

The force of the expression, ' the Holy Innocents,' came home to him more and more every moment.

John Ramsay had only got as far as innocence yet. It was a step in the right direction, but it was only a step.

He had yet to learn that there is something better than innocence, something higher, firmer, more enduring.

He had yet to learn that man cannot live for ever in the garden of Eden, and that moreover, if he could, it would not be the highest state of existence.

But the thread of his reflections is

broken, the sermon is over, the Benediction is said, and Gillie is at the bottom of the pew, carefully collecting all his precious little bits of white paper.

CHAPTER VIII.

THE TWO FRIENDS IN SOCIETY.

THE next day, as Mr. Ramsay and his
little companion were returning home from
an afternoon ramble, Gillie descried with
great excitement the marks of recent
carriage-wheels on the gravel-sweep.

Mr. Ramsay did not appear to share
his pleasurable interest, but with an exclamation that sounded like dismay, hurried
on into the house.

Gillie followed, and, finding him standing transfixed at the hall-table, pushed forward to see what he was looking at.

'Take care!' exclaimed his uncle.

'What is it?' said Gillie. 'A wasp?'

'Something much worse,' muttered John Ramsay.

'Worse?' exclaimed the child, peering under his uncle's elbow. 'Is it an adder?'

But to John Ramsay the thing lying on the hall-table was something far worse than either a wasp or an adder. It was a visiting-card!—indeed, *two* visiting-cards: a small one with one name, a larger one with several.

In his eyes a terrible meaning was attached to those small white and apparently inoffensive bits of pasteboard lying there on the old oak-table. It was a representative misery: a coming event that cast its shadow before. It meant—— Well, what did it *not* mean?

It meant that his neighbours had found

him out, that the county was beginning to call upon him. It meant—worst horror of all!—that the visit would have to be returned.

It meant society, and small talk, and ladies, and everything else that his whole soul shrank from.

'What *is* to be done?' he muttered to himself. 'What a dreadful thing!'

He took the innocent white things up in his hands, touching them warily, fearfully, gingerly, as if he thought they would burn, with a dismayed and disgusted ex pression on his countenance.

He almost dropped the biggest in his consternation, as his eye lighted on the names of not only a lady, but of *two* daughters.

'Too bad,' he muttered to himself. 'I must go up to town at once.'

'Uncle John,' said little Gillie's voice at his elbow, 'why do you look so wretchable when you look at those cards?'

'Gillie,' said his uncle solemnly, '*those cards will have to be returned.*'

This fearful announcement did not appear to affect Gillie in the way its emphatic delivery deserved.

'Give them back?' he said. 'Oh no, Uncle John, I don't think you need. I dare say the lady what left them has got plenty more.'

'I've no doubt she has,' muttered Mr. Ramsay bitterly. 'Look here, Gillie,' he said, facing round upon the little boy, 'that *visit* will have to be returned, and that's all about it. We shall have to go and *see* these people. Don't you understand?'

' Oh, what fun ! ' exclaimed Gillie.
' *When* shall we go—to-morrow ? '

For the first time Mr. Ramsay felt
himself out of sympathy with his little
nephew. But such a feeling could not last :
Gillie's anxiety to go and see a new house
and new people prevailed.

A sense of duty to his neighbours, also,
told Mr. Ramsay the visit must be returned
some day, and, therefore, the sooner it was
over the better.

Accordingly, the carriage was ordered
one afternoon, and Mr. Ramsay and Gillie
started on their expedition.

It was fine when they set out, but the
weather clouded over, and it turned into
a thoroughly wet afternoon.

Mr. Ramsay's hopes of finding the
people out fell to zero.

So did his spirits, as they drove up to the door.

And yet he little knew what lay before him.

The house was quite full: a large party having been brought down from London for Whitsuntide.

John Ramsay little knew, either, what risks he ran.

Under such circumstances a country neighbour sometimes fares very badly.

For it is a sad fact, though a true one, that you often find the worst manners in what is called the best society.

Any one who has ever fallen foul of a 'clique' will endorse this opinion.

The selfishness of a 'clique,' and its disregard for the feelings of others, is proverbial.

It is at the same time the pleasantest

form of society for those within it, but *tant pis* for those outside.

It has its own set, its own jokes, its own ways of viewing people, its own standard of judgment; even its own language. Or, at any rate, the constant re-iteration of words and phrases which no one else understands in the sense in which they have come to be used have, by degrees, almost formed a language. It is, at any rate, Greek to the uninitiated; so that at once makes it a language for the few.

A clique of this kind is often downright rude to what they consider an intruder; to any one who dares to venture into their charmed circle—any one whom they do not know, whose face they are unaccustomed to see.

So that John Ramsay, as I said before,

S

ran a greater risk than he knew of, when he paid his visit that day.

Let me at once say, however, that the circle into which he and his little nephew were about to be ushered was not a clique of the kind I have been describing.

His advent was rather welcome. It was a wet day. Only a few of the younger men had ventured out for a walk: the bulk of the party was at home.

A visitor was not an unpleasant variety on a dull afternoon.

And then John Ramsay was rather a hero in the county.

His fortune had, of course, been ex-aggerated, and he was looked upon as a man of really fabulous wealth.

His history, too, interested his neigh-bours; and his curious ways, his unso-ciability, the hermit nature of his existence all his life, of which they had heard, interested them still more.

The solitary character always exercises a certain kind of charm. Stop short of being eccentric, and your lonely life will always have an attraction for others.

The announcement of ' Mr. Ramsay ' was really quite an excitement.

It was tea-time, and the party was sitting in groups about the room. There were three or four middle-aged and elderly men ; and *all* the rest were ladies !

Conceive poor John Ramsay's feelings.

To his blurred physical vision, as he entered, every seat in the room seemed occupied ; and to his mental vision, a frivolous talking woman sat on every chair !

Lady Follett, the hostess, came forward and received him with great cordiality ;

sat him comfortably down, offered him tea, regretted her husband was not at home, and in every way tried to entertain him and to draw him out.

Not very successfully.

There are some people who pride themselves on being able to 'get on' with a stiff or silent person, whom every one else calls 'difficult to get on with.'

'I know people *say* he is difficult to get on with, but *I* always get on very well with him. He is always very nice to *me*,' are sentences no doubt familiar to the reader, from the lips of his divers acquaintances.

Lady Follett was free from petty little vanities of this kind; but she was a really kind-hearted woman, and liked to make every one round her happy and at their case. She had not, however, often had so tough a subject to work upon as John Ramsay, and her heart soon began to fail her.

Leaving her for the present to her arduous task, we will take a turn round the room, and give our attention to some of the other people.

Passing by two or three ladies, who, with heads close together and lowered voices, are evidently talking gossip, we will join a group, gathered round a lady, Mrs. L'Estrange by name, who appears to be holding forth to her listeners at some length.

Mrs. L'Estrange is a lady who will talk by the hour about herself, her concerns, and her domestic management.

Everything Mrs. L'Estrange does—according to her own account—is right and successful and far in advance of other people.

Her children are the best mannered, the best behaved, and the best dressed.

Yet she spends very much less on their dress than do many others whose children do not look nearly so nice.

There is a system of management in her nursery, a care of the clothes, a putting-by and a passing-on from one child to a younger; which produces all these happy results.

Her own dress is managed in the same satisfactory and successful way.

Almost everything she wears is made at home, and yet her things never have a 'home-made' look.

Many women at three times the expense look only half as well.

She has a good maid, it is true. But

then who made her what she is? In the same way she has a good nurse. But then who trained her? As the head of an establishment is responsible for all failure; so is it glorified by all success.

Mrs. L'Estrange's nursery—she lives in London—is always out in the park by nine o'clock. No one else succeeds in getting *their* nursery out till half-past; some not till a quarter to ten.

While admitting that she is no doubt 'lucky in her servants,' she manages to convey to her listeners that her nurse was a 'mere girl' when she came to her, and that she had had some trouble to get her into 'her ways'; at least, it had taken some time. The effect a woman like Mrs. L'Estrange produces on others, is curious to observe. It varies according to their natures. Some are profoundly depressed

by her, believe her, admire her, and feel
their own inferiority.

But in others it rouses very opposite
feelings.

'Humble-minded and modest people,'
says a writer of to-day, 'are rather disposed to feel an innocent admiration for a
man who is perfectly satisfied with himself
and his doings . . . and take it for granted
that he has adequate reasons for his self-
complacency.'

Poor little Mrs. Singleton, who was sitting near Mrs. L'Estrange, felt her defi-
ciencies sadly, and wished she was as good
a manager. Her nurse really would make
nothing. She had to have all the best
frocks made out. And *she* never could
get her nursery out early. She had been
trying in vain for years. She wished she
could, etc., etc.

But had Lady Plumptre, who was out of earshot, been in Mrs. Singleton's place, the result would have been very different. *She* would have dealt with Mrs. L'Estrange very differently.

And for this reason—

'I have noticed,' says the same writer quoted above, 'that the sins to which men are specially sensitive in others are precisely the sins to which they are themselves most inclined. . . . Other people's vanity and conceit are offences against our good opinion of ourselves; and the more modest we are the less likely we are to be wounded.'

Those who inflict these mortifications on others may do it from a sort of ignorant selfishness: more so, perhaps, than from an actual want of Christian charity; but every one who witnesses this kind of thing must feel an inclination indignantly to deprecate any one's right to make other people, and especially humble-minded and modest people, feel small and uncomfortable.

Sitting not far from Mrs. L'Estrange and her auditors is old Lord George Norton.

Lord George is afflicted with a peculiarity which is getting sadly common, and is now by no means confined to elderly people.

I allude to the propensity of forgetting at the crisis of a story or of a conversation the name of the person on whom its whole interest hinges; so that the story or the conversation comes abruptly to an end at the prime moment.

This propensity is very much on the increase. Hardly a dinner party now, that

it does not sooner or later occur, and conversation become thereby paralysed.

It is becoming quite a vocation in
society to supply missing names.

Lord George has just come to a dead
stop.

He was telling a capital story, and was
working up most successfully to his point,
when the whole thing collapsed for want of
a name, a want which every one is now en-
deavouring to supply ; but as yet in vain.

He will not go on until he has remembered it, and ransacks his brain, giving
little hints now and then to his long-suffer-
ing listeners which do not throw much
light upon the subject.

'Oh, you'd know it the moment I said
it, you all know the man as well as possible. Bah ! I know his name as well as I
know my own.'

Failing that way he tries personal description.

'Tall fellow, you know.   Dark, with an
eye-glass.'

Every one suggests a friend who answers
to the description.

There are unfortunately so many tall
dark fellows with eye-glasses.

Each suggestion makes him more
furious.   One and. all are so far removed
from the person of whom he is thinking ;
and ruin, to his mental eye, the point of
the story.

Prevailed upon at last to continue without the name, he starts again—

'Well, it can't be helped—I suppose I
shall remember it by-and-by.   At any rate
this fellow went down to his place last
autumn, down to——'

Here Lord George is brought to

another dead stop by having forgotten the name of the place, and the conversation is again paralysed.

' Oh, you all know the place!—down in Shropshire, beautiful place, famous for its timber. Dear, dear! what is the name of the place? I shall forget my own name next. Why it's close to——'

He is now getting further and further involved by forgetting the name of the post-town. He tries the parliamentary borough for which the nameless one sits, but he has forgotten that too. He makes a dash at the big manufacturing town which is within a drive, but that name has also escaped him ; neither can he remember the manufacture for which the town is celebrated, and which might have been a clue. This time nothing will persuade him to go on. He remains wrapt in thought ;

getting deeper and deeper into a web of entanglement, in his vain chase after the missing names.

His auditors are now wearied, and turn to other topics. A new conversation is started, and has reached a most interesting point, when there is a sudden shout from Lord George.

He has remembered the man's name! *And* the name of his place! Also the borough, the manufacturing town, *and* the manufacture!

A perfect flood of recollection has come over him.

'Of course!' he exclaims · 'Talbot of Blaymoor—I knew I should come to it at last. Well, Talbot went down—' but, alas, it is too late! The interest of his auditors is not again to be roused. To Lord George

himself his story, under the light of recovered memory, wears a new and brilliant
aspect, but to every one else it is a weariness.
Their attention has been diverted into
other channels.

He tell his story, but it falls quite flat.

He then proceeds to the links of evi-
dence in the chain of association.

He relates with delight the processes of
thought by which he arrived at the missing
names, and laughs in fits as he recalls and
recounts them.   But no one else is the least
amused.   Leaving him to this enjoyment,
let us move on to another part of the room,
and give our attention to Colonel Cavendish,
a man with whom no doubt the reader is,
to his cost, acquainted.   Colonel Cavendish always knows best on every subject,
from the deepest to the most trifling.

His judgment is, in his own eyes, final on all points.

He not only lays down the law, but he disputes any one's right to venture to disagree with him; and his powers of argument and of contradiction are of the most unfailing order. The two combined, form his highest, if not his only, idea of conversation.

The effect he, and such as he, produce on a party—when all have become thoroughly aware of his character and have suffered from it—is unfortunate, but inevitable.

Even the weakest and least pugnacious is roused, and *every one* becomes argumentative and self-asserting.

Look at him now, wandering with his cup of tea in his hand from one group to another, and observe how, from whatever

part of the room he may happen at the
moment to be, a discussion or an argument at once springs up.

You hear points, so insignificant as to
be *beneath* discussion, being discussed with
an ardour and a warmth which you know
they could not evoke but for every one's
knowledge of, and rebellion against, the
nature of the man who raises them.

Even little Mrs. Singleton, who was so
crushed just now by Mrs. L'Estrange's
superiority, is fired to some sort of self-
assertion.

The worm will turn.

From the tea-table where she is sitting,
and which he has just reached, come now
such scraps of conversation as these—

'I am confident we turned to the left.
I feel sure it was not to the right.' 'No,
indeed, it was not on Monday; it was on

Tuesday. I am positive it was not Monday,' etc., etc.

In ·the words of the poet she unconsciously makes her protest—

   'Though syllogisms hang not on my tongue,
    I am not surely *always* in the wrong ;
    'Tis hard if all is false that I advance,
    A fool must now and then be right—by chance.'

Meantime, poor Lady Follett has not even been enjoying the glory of feeling she was 'getting on,' with a person 'difficult to get on with.'

John Ramsay had been getting stiffer and stiffer ever since he sat down.

She had tried almost every subject, but he was really impossible. He was so unsuggestive that each topic was quickly exhausted. She had come to an end now, and silence was reigning between them.

Poor man ! He was very miserable ;

and he saw no chance of getting away. And then, unfortunately, he was within ear-shot of that subdued conversation which we mentioned before, and to which the reader did not stop to listen.

A flood of London gossip was thus being poured upon him. Marriages were being announced, commented on, talked over, in the very way that was likely to confirm him in his opinion of women being talking, frivolous creatures. 'Is it a good marriage?' 'Is he rich?' etc., etc., were the sentences continually ringing in his ears. The talkers were really what he, most unfairly, imagined every woman to be.

And then little Gillie, to whom he had clung at first as a drowning man clutches at a straw, had strayed from him, and was enjoying himself immensely. He was being made much of, given tea, talked to, questioned, applauded; and was making friends everywhere.

Lady Follett tried to create a diversion.

She made a sign to her married daughter to come to her assistance.

'If any one can make him talk, it will be Adeline,' she said to herself.

This was, as it proved, an unfortunate move. For Adeline was another instance of Mr. Ramsay's pet aversions. She was his typical woman, in short; expecting little attentions, exacting small acts of homage, and looking upon admiration as her due.

She was the beauty of the family, and had been spoilt and made much of all her life, first by her family and then by her husband. Rather bored, but confident in her own powers, she obeyed her mother's signal, and advanced to John Ramsay's side.

In so doing she dropped her work; whether purposely or not I cannot 'tell. Needless to say Mr. Ramsay did not stir. Somewhat nettled, she picked it up herself, and sat down.

Her manner was slightly affected, and gave an idea of unreality.

'I look upon you as a most fortunate man, Mr. Ramsay,' she began, '*much* to be envied. What a delightful thing to have accomplished one's life's aim! And how *few* people do!'

John Ramsay felt as if turned to stone.

The manner, the implied compliment, the suddenness of the whole thing, and the sense of how utterly she was in the dark, how completely mistaken, overpowered him.

He made no answer.

That failed.

She tried something else.

'How nice for you to have that sweet little boy with you! What a *lovely* child he is! What eyes! And what a complexion! And then he is so amusing and so angelic.'

If any subject could have roused John Ramsay it would have been this one. But the way in which it was broached shut him up. First of all he was so afraid Gillie, who was not far off, might overhear this torrent of fulsome flattery—and to have Gillie's unconsciousness destroyed would have been the height of misfortune in John Ramsay's eyes. It was one of the things in which he most delighted. And then, how could he speak to this trifler, this outsider, of what lay so near his heart? How could he tell her of all that that child was to him ?—of all that he was daily and hourly learning at his little teacher's feet?

He was quite unequal to the occasion. The very thought of the child brought a lump into his throat.

Fortunately Adeline finished her sentence by asking the little boy's name, and Mr. Ramsay answered the question.

Gillie, catching the sound of his name, came running up, thinking his uncle had called him. 'Did you want me, Uncle John?' he said, in his pretty little coaxing way.

'I *always* want you, my dear, dear little fellow,' whispered Mr. Ramsay, as the child nestled up to him. But out loud he only said, 'No, Gillie, I was telling this lady your name.'

Adeline now turned her attention to the pretty boy.

'Before I married,' she said, putting on an unnecessary infantine way of speaking, as if Gillie were three years old, 'I used to have a little, teeny, tiny garden here, of my very, very own.'

'Did you?' said Gillie, clapping his hands with delight. 'Oh! are there any old ruins of it left?'

The laughter that followed this *naïf* remark nettled our young friend, already provoked by her non-success with Mr. Ramsay. She had married at nineteen, and rather liked to think, though she had been married several years, that she was nineteen still.

She left her seat and strolled towards the open piano. Lord George now put in his oar.

'Are you fond of music, Mr. Ramsay?' he said. 'I have no doubt some of the ladies will give us some.'

'No, I can't say I am,' answered Mr. Ramsay, bluntly; thinking with horror of an instrumental piece, an Italian song with shakes, or a sentimental English ballad; and with still greater horror of being expected to say something to the performer when it was over.

Lord George was so astonished and nonplussed that he moved away without saying anything more, and gave up any further attempt to assist in the entertainment of so very peculiar a person.

'I must get out of this,' said John Ramsay to himself. But it was impossible to move till Gillie had done his tea, and that event seemed still a very remote possibility.

However, the happy moment came at last, and in some sort of fashion Mr.

Ramsay managed to rise from his seat, and to take his leave.

Lord George and another man came with him to the door to see him off, an attention which John Ramsay felt indeed to be quite superfluous.

But it had suddenly occurred to Lord George that he and Mr. Ramsay might possibly have a subject in common in the shape of a friend in India, whom he thought Mr. Ramsay might have known there.

It was not likely in any case that Mr. Ramsay would have met the person in question, so it did not matter; but it is unnecessary to say that when it came to the point, Lord George could not remember his friend's name; so the attempt proved a failure.

Mr. Ramsay did not wait to give him

time to search for it, but got into the carriage, and drove off, leaving Lord George standing in the hall, wrapt in thought, trying by every means to recall the name to his memory.

Turning at last to the other man, Mr. Fraser, Lord George deplores his want of success, and fears he must give it up for the present.

He is, however, full of hope.

The name, he feels confident, will recur to him sooner or later; most probably in the middle of the night. Should it do so, he promises Mr. Fraser that he will come into his room and wake him up to tell it to him. And Mr. Fraser earnestly implores him not.

Meanwhile, as the carriage speeds along John Ramsay has leant back with a sigh of relief, and, throwing his arm round

Gillie, has drawn the child closer to him.

'We won't pay any more visits, Gillie,' he said. 'We are so much happier alone together, you and I. We don't want anybody else.'

'*Wasn't* it fun?' said Gillie enthusiastically.

CHAPTER IX.

HOW IS IT ALL TO END?

THE return to the still world of child-life was most soothing and refreshing to John Ramsay after that peep into society.

The simplicity and guilelessness of child-nature seemed to him more attractive than ever.

The contrast between the atmosphere in which the child continually dwelt, and that of which he had had experience that day, was ever in his mind.

There was to John Ramsay such an un-reality about it all. That, he told himself, was what he hated so about it ; that it was which was so distasteful to him.

False smiles, empty compliments, un-meaning speeches ; the expression of unfelt sentiments.

How *real* the child was in comparison !

He never said anything he did not mean ; he never talked for effect, nor with an object.

What he said came straight from his heart. Take that young person,—it was so he inwardly designated the great Adeline ! —for instance ; and compare her artificiality with Gillie's unconsciousness.

The fear of his ever losing it seemed to him a greater disaster than ever.

He thought of Gillie's *naïf* remark, and the effect it had produced : how his simple words and earnest manner had made what she was saying, and the way in which she was saying it, seem hollow and unreal.

His mind strayed on to the thought of

that subdued conversation he had heard going on near him in the pauses of his spasmodic talk with Lady Follett ; and of the ' tone ' of the speakers.

How poor, he thought, how unworthy were their ways of thinking and judging !

His unfortunate juxtaposition to those gossiping ladies had had a disastrous effect upon him.

They had in his eyes coloured, or rather blackened, the whole atmosphere ; and made him inclined to judge the whole of society by a part ; the many by the few, as people so often unfairly do.

He half felt himself he was being a little hard even on those particular ladies, for he muttered presently that there was no harm exactly in those people ; it was not the people themselves, it was the atmosphere in which they dwelt.   It was

the worldly and hollow tone of their judgments and opinions.   They took altogether
a false view of the meaning of life, and of
the true and relative value of things with
them : the question was not ' Is he good ? '
but ' Is he rich ? ' Not ' What is he like ? '
but ' What is he worth ? '   To this he
could testify.

The reiterated enquiry, ' Is it a good
marriage ? ' had meant *not* ' Is he a good
man, a man into whose keeping a parent
might safely confide a child,' but good in
the sense of ' Has he of this world's good ?
Has he much good of this kind laid up for
many years?   Can he eat, drink, and be
merry ? '

Where a person, then, is thus valued, is
judged not by what he *is*, but by what he
has, where, John Ramsay asked himself, is
there any place for right judgments and

high standards? He did not spare himself, or for one moment think himself
better than they. Poor John Ramsay did
not feel inclined to say to *any one*, 'Stand
back; I am holier than thou.' He had
been all his life, he told himself, quite as
worldly as they, quite as mistaken in life's
meaning; his standards and aims quite as
poor, quite as unworthy, as theirs.

For anything that, by shutting out the
unseen and eternal, causes absorption in
the seen and temporal, *is* worldliness; and,
viewed in that light, his life and theirs were
alike worldly, because they were lived at
a low level, and with a poor standard;
levels and standards that seem so unworthy
when contrasted with the thought of what
a grand thing may be made of life, as
some have done, and are doing still;
levels and standards that seem still more

U

unworthy when 'we take our Bibles, and read what Christ said and did, and reflect that we are called by His Name.'

They, like him, were not making the most of their lives. They were wasting them.

They were created for higher objects; they were worthy of better things. On them, as on him, the crust of earthliness had come down, gathered over their better selves, and buried their higher nature.

That the child should ever grow up to have ignoble aims; should come to lower his standard to the level of the world around him; should live to conform a higher tone to the tone of those about him; was to John Ramsay a thought that he shrank from.

So once before, in the church of the

old county-town, he had shrunk from the thought of a day ever coming when Gillie should have the aspirations of his higher nature buried, like his, under the weight of absorption in unworthy things.

Then, as now, it seemed to him it would be better that *anything* should happen to the child than that his purity and innocence should be in any way marred or sullied.

Then, as now, innocence was the pivot round which all his thoughts turned.

One day, when Gillie, childlike, said something about what he should do when he was 'grown-up,' Mr. Ramsay gave a little shudder, and, with an irresistible impulse, drew the boy nearer to him with a protecting movement, as if shielding him from the future, and said : ' *Never* grow

U 2

up, Gillie; always remain as you are, my dear, dear little fellow.'

'Never grow up!' repeated Gillie, rather startled. 'Why, then I should have to *die*, shouldn't I? Do you want me to *die*, Uncle John?'

Uncle John made a gesture of horrified dissent.

'Of course, I know I must die some day,' said Gillie, in rather a mournful voice; 'but I think I would rather die *after* I'm grown up; I'd rather be a man first. It isn't wrong to say that, is it?' he said wistfully, putting his pretty little face close to his uncle's.

'No, no, my child,' murmured John Ramsay huskily.

As the child spoke a new thought had come into his mind, and he wanted to think it out.

So he kissed him very tenderly, and told him to run out and play, and not to think any more of what he had said.

That Gillie should leave his purity and innocence behind him, had hitherto been to him a most painful thought; but it seemed now hardly less painful and unnatural that his little life should be prematurely cut short.

What might not the fruit of a bud of so much promise be? What might not be the development of so precious a germ?

Gillie might become a noble man. He might be one of those who pass unscathed through the fire of this world's temptations; he might refuse the evil and choose the good—nay, more: he might one day be a blessing to all around him, a strength and a stay to others.

It did not seem to him now, after all,

as if death in childhood was the only solu-
tion of the difficulties of life. He had got
beyond the thought of innocence.

He had made another step.

Time, meanwhile, was speeding on.

The accounts from the Rectory varied
very little from day to day; but the crisis
was approaching.

In a few days, at latest, the fever would
have run its course; and then the question
of strength would decide the rest.

Once or twice lately the thought, 'What
if there should be a fatal termination to this
illness?' had flitted through John Ramsay's
mind, and sudden horror had seized him at
the thought of the bitter grief that might
be coming on the tender-hearted child.
But the thought had been so painful that
he had resolutely put it away, and was
content to enjoy the happy uncertainty;

to let day by day slip away, and the
golden present flow on, without thought
of what was to come after.

But one evening when Gillie came to
wish him good-night the child suddenly
said—

'Isn't to-day the last. day of June,
Uncle John?'

'Yes, I think it is—the 30th; there are
only thirty days in June. Why?'

'Why, then it is the first of July to-
morrow!' exclaimed Gillie.

'Certainly it is, my dear child; but
what of that?'

'"What of that?"' said the little boy,
in tones of tremulous excitement. 'Why,
Uncle John, don't you see, Puppy will soon
be getting quite well again; for almost
directly the three weeks will be over?
Even to-morrow we shall be able to say

" In a day or two more we shall see Puppy again." '

Mr. Ramsay sat very quiet for a long time after the child had gone to bed.

It was not a happy train of thought which his parting words had set going. He must face the truth now.

The three weeks were over. His happy life with the child was at an end.

What had not the child done for him in these blessed three weeks?

What a world of pure happiness they had opened out to him! What an insight they had given him into things unknown before! Yes; the dream was over; the awakening had come.

This bright daily participation in child-life was at an end.

It had been very sweet while it lasted; but it was over now.

It had been so sweet because the child so depended on him; looked to him so confidently for sympathy and affection; made him so naturally the centre of all his interests. Yes; he must let all this go.

He must give him up to those who had a real right to him.

He had none.

'Soon we shall be able to say : " In a day or two more we shall see Puppy again." '

The ring of joy in the dear little voice; the sparkle of excitement in the eye; the look of love and pleasure in the beaming face : all had brought home to John Ramsay what he had allowed himself to forget—that another had a right to his darling; a far greater right than he.

And now what would happen to him —what would become of him ?

Would he become again the weary unsatisfied being he had been before? Would that horrible hardness come back again—that coldness and indifference and selfishness which he now looked back upon with loathing and abhorrence?

He had got thus far in his sad meditations, when there came a low tap at the library door.

PART III.

NEMESIS

CHAPTER I.

CONSEQUENCES.

'Our deeds still travel with us from afar,
  And what we have leen, makes us what we are.'

Consequences are unpitying.—GEORGE ELIOT.

SURPRISED at such an interruption at so unwonted an hour, Mr. Ramsay turned his head sharply round as he said 'Come in,' and saw Mrs. Pryor standing in the doorway.

There was something so unusual in her whole demeanour that he exclaimed 'Good God! Mrs. Pryor! what is the matter? Is there'—struck with a sudden panic—'is there anything wrong with the child?'

'No, sir,' answered Mrs. Pryor; ' but there is terrible news from the Rectory.'

'Is—is—my brother dead?' faltered John Ramsay, turning pale.

'They say he can't live through the night, sir,' sobbed Mrs. Pryor. 'Oh dear! oh dear! how is that darling child to be told? It'll break his heart—that's what it will do. He'll ask me, when I go to him in the morning, how his father is, and what *shall* I say?'

And Mrs. Pryor fairly broke down, and cried bitterly.

Some one else's eyes were dim too.

'It ought to be broken to him to-night, sir; indeed it ought.'

'Very well, Mrs. Pryor,' said Mr. Ramsay, in a voice which he in vain endeavoured to render steady, ' then you had better go up and prepare him.   He will not be asleep yet.'

But Mrs. Pryor shrank back in dismay.

She *couldn't*! She *couldn't*, she exclaimed, clasping her hands together. How could she? She who knew better than any one *how* the child loved his father, *what* a father he was, and what a tender heart the child had. No, no! She couldn't tell him. Mr. Ramsay *must* not ask her to.

'Certainly,' thought John Ramsay to himself, as he looked at her quivering face, and listened to her impassioned description of the home and the family, as she had known both for so many years ; ' certainly, if the child is to have the terrible news broken to him *thus*, then some one else must do it.'

He did not allow himself to pursue the thought further, or to consider what the alternative must be, or he could not have controlled himself as he did, nor have spoken in that quiet voice of unnatural calm.

' Very well, Mrs. Pryor,' he said, ' I will not ask you to.'

And then a very extraordinary thing happened.

Mr. Ramsay got up from his chair, and assumed the offiee of consoler as if it were the most matter-of-course thing in the world.

He took Mrs. Pryor's hand, and spoke kindly and gently to her, begging her to go to bed and try to get some sleep.

' You will come and tell me,' he said, ' when the message comes '—he paused, for the thought brought a spasm into his throat—' to-morrow ! '

He opened the door for her with an unwonted civility, which was *not* civility, but a real expression of kindliness and sympathy, and then returned to his seat, and covered his face with his hands.

'I shall come to some conclusion in a minute or two,' he said presently, half out-loud, ' but I must collect my thoughts first.'

But far from collecting them, he found them straying farther and farther away.

He found himself thinking of the life that was passing away ; of that unknown brother, his only blood relation.

He had unconsciously formed an idea of him from what he had gathered from things the child had said about him, and from the child himself, who was the result of his training and education.

That loyalty towards himself, which had

X

so struck him once before, came back to his recollection now.

That loyalty which had shrunk from poisoning his children's minds against their uncle, and had never let them guess how deeply he had been disappointed in him; that had concealed for them that the home-coming so long looked forward to—had proved as much a sham and a deception as had the vision of a loving and tender-hearted relation, who would beautify their young lives by his love and kindness.

How different the past three weeks might have been if a word had ever been said to little Gillie, which would have shattered his ideal! But the father had never told the child anything which would have made him do otherwise than accept him, John Ramsay, at once as the same loving man he was himself.

And it was *this* man, the much and deservedly loved, the much needed, who was going, if not already gone, while *he*, unnecessary to any one, was left!

He found himself picturing the home the housekeeper had just described with such unconscious pathos, rendered blank and void by the absence of that central figure.

And, then, like a cold blast, swept over John Ramsay the conviction, held at bay for so long, that it was all his doing, all his fault.

The happiness of that home had been blasted by his hand.

It was no use deceiving himself; no use making excuses; *he* was the cause of it all.

He knew it all the time the housekeeper was speaking; but he would not let himself dwell on the thought.

He could have implored her at the time to stop; to spare him; to cease with her vivid picture of the home he had blasted; the circle he had rent asunder; the hearts he had made desolate!

Yes. He was the dark shadow, he was the cause of it all.

'No,' said a rebellious voice within him; 'it is unfair to say so. I did not do anything knowingly—I did not realise —I did not think—Am I my brother's keeper?'

In vain. Not a committed sin, perhaps, but the hard cold sin of omission; the want of setting self aside, and putting himself into other people's places; the fatal habit of looking at life *only* from his own point of view; the cruel sin of selfishness.

And now Nemesis was at hand.

The thought he had put away before must be faced now.

He must go and prepare the child.

This was the punishment that now lay before him. Who else was there to do it?

Upon the being whom he would have shielded from the slightest breath of sorrow he had himself brought the desolation that was coming, and he must tell him it was at the door.

He must see innocence suffer, and know all the while it was his own fault.

He rebelled fiercely against the inevitable ; told himself that the retribution was out of all proportion to the offence, all unknowing and indirect as it was.

But ' the terrible law of cause and effeet is inexorable, and wrong-doing inevitably brings its own punishment, and that not to the wrong-doer alone. The tendency of selfishness and wrong is to develop misery on all who come within its influence, and our deeds must necessarily carry their terrible consequences; consequences that are hardly ever confined to ourselves.'

They are not always, indeed, so apparent as in John Ramsay's case.

'For,' continues George Eliot, 'there is much pain that is quite noiseless; and vibrations, which make human agonies, are often a mere whisper in the roar of hurrying existence.'

There are moments in life when we wish we had no feeling; when we would gladly so harden ourselves that we might 'feel no more'; when the heavens above are as brass, and all the earth around is in darkness; when our prayer, 'wild in its fervour as the Syro-Phœnician woman's, seems to have the same reply—He answered her not a word.'

Such a moment was on John Ramsay now.

'Oh God!' he cried. 'I *cannot* do it. How *can* I? How *can* I?'

He gasped for breath. He went to the window, threw it open, and leaned out.

But the calm beauty of the June night did nothing for him.

Rather the scene before him made him more wretched.

Everything he looked at spoke to him of the child-spirit, which had glorified life to him during the past three weeks, and transformed all which had once seemed to him so dreary and disappointing.

The gardens before him teemed with his little presence. The now silent terrace seemed still to echo with the sound of his dancing footsteps, and of his merry laugh.

Dancing footsteps, and merry laugh, which, he told himself, would be heard now no more!

The night was hot and oppressive: not a breath of air was stirring.

Neither mentally nor physically was any relief to be found. He closed the window.

' I *must* go up to him,' he said to himself once or twice ; but still he did not move.

The thought unnerved him quite.

But at last, with a set face that told of a formed resolution, he walked into the hall, lit a bedroom candle, and went slowly upstairs.

. . . .

The large oak staircase echoed drearily to his halting footsteps. It looked weird and desolate by the flicker of the bedroom candle.

He paused for a minute at the top of the stairs; turned down the passage; paused again; stood stock still for a minute at the half-open door of the little bedroom, and, closing his lips firmly together, pushed it open and went in.

A great feeling of relief came down upon his spirit when he realised, by the silence that reigned in the room, that the child was already asleep.

It was a respite anyhow; and John Ramsay drew a long breath, and then advanced very softly to the bedside, and, shading the light of the candle with one hand, stood looking down upon the little sleeper.

In deep contrast to the storm of thoughts which had been sweeping over him, was the calm, rapt repose of the slumbering child. Few things bring such a sense of quiet and peace.

He lay with one arm outside the coverlid; the other grasping tightly his last cherished possession.

His bright hair was tublmed all over the pillow, and his rosy lips were parted with a smile.

Was he dreaming on this hot oppressive night of—

> . . . cool forests far away,
> And of rosy happy children laughing merrily at play,
> Coming home through green lanes bearing
> Trailing boughs of blooming may.

Long, John Ramsay stood there gazing, drinking in the calm and repose which the sight was calculated to inspire.

And now what was he to do?

Rouse him from his sleep to sorrow? Wake him up to grief?

Recall him from his dreams of happiness to the cold realities of life, and the shadow of approaching trouble?

No ! a thousand times, no.

' Lord, if he sleep, he shall do well,' he whispered.

With an indescribable feeling of love and pity, he bent over the little sleeper ; bent lower and lower till he touched the child's forehead with his trembling lips.

' Sleep on, my fair child,' he said, ' and dream bright dreams once more.'

And Gillie smiled in his sleep, and murmured his father's name.

CHAPTER II.

THE MESSAGE FROM THE RECTORY.

JOHN RAMSAY passed a terrible night, tossing restlessly about: one moment longing for the night to be over, and the next shrinking from the morning's inevitable approach.

He was astir early, hoping to be down before Gillie. But the child was beforehand with him. He could hear, as he descended the stairs, the merry laugh somewhere outside in the court-yard, and the eager chatter with the footman among their live treasures.

Mr. Ramsay sat down, and tried to prepare himself for what lay before him.

He began to think over what he was going to say; how he should begin; how he should—— Oh! that merry laugh! There it was again! How it was *ringing* through the court-yard! How clear! How musical it was!

He must be quick. At any moment the message might come from the Rectory, and the child *must* be prepared.

Again the happy laugh rang out in the summer stillness. He must go and stop it. He must go and lay a chill hand on the laughing lips, and bid all joy flee away. It must be done.

And, as in a dream, he walked to the end of the passage, where a window looked out on the court-yard.

'Gillie,' he called through the open window, and his voice sounded to himself hollow and strange, 'Gillie, come into

the dining-room ; I want to speak to you.'
And, without waiting for an answer, he
hurried back into the dining-room, and
sat down.   His heart was beating loud
and fast.   He fixed his eyes nervously on
the door by which the child would enter.
He had not to wait long.   The door was
presently pushed open, and Gillie entered—
joy dancing in his eyes; his arms filled
with something he was cherishing with the
greatest care and tenderness.

'Oh, Uncle John!—Uncle John! look
here!   Only see!'

And in a moment four little kittens were
in Mr. Ramsay's lap, and their transported
owner was kneeling at his side, with his
bright joyous eyes uplifted to his grave
grey face.   'Oh! ain't they lovely! ain't
they beautiful!   Four of them, and all
mine!   Just born, or, at least, only last

night. The butler wanted to drown them, cruel man! but I said he should not till I had asked you; and you won't say they're to be drowned, Uncle John, I *know*, if I ask you not, *will* you?'

And the trusting brown eyes were raised full of appeal.

Mr. Ramsay turned away; he could not bear to meet their expression.

But he murmured something about that 'if there were *forty* instead of four, no one should touch them if the child did not wish it.'

'I said so!' said Gillie joyfully, rising from his kneeling position, and throwing his arms round his uncle's neck. 'Dear, dear Uncle John; I knew you'd be kind to the dear little kitties, like you *always* are. And they'll want to be kept *very* warm, you know; so I think two might sleep in your bed, and two in mine. Don't you? **I'm** *very* busy this morning,' he added; ' so can you let me go back now, **if** you don't want me this very minute? '

John Ramsay writhed in his chair.

How lay a shadow on that bright face? How bring a rain of tears to those dear speaking eyes?

He caught the child in his arms, and called him his ' poor little fellow; his ' dear, *dear* little boy,' over and over again.

Surprised at this unusual display of emotion, Gillie grew a little suspicious. ' What's the matter? ' he said wistfully : ' why!—why! —why, you're *crying*, Uncle John. Oh dear! what is the matter? ' And the sympathetic brown eyes filled too.

John Ramsay tried to speak, but something in his throat prevented a word from becoming audible.

And in the short silence that followed, came through the open window—borne from the distant village on the wings of the summer breezes—the single stroke of a church bell! . . .

Mr. Ramsay started, turned deadly white, and grasped with both hands the arms of his chair.

'Put the kittens away,' he said faintly, 'and come here.'

'Gillie, my *darling*!' he exclaimed, with a sudden outburst of passionate tenderness, clasping the child in his arms. 'Listen to what I am going to tell you.'

'Hark, Uncle John!' interrupted the little boy in a tone of eager excitement, disengaging himself from his uncle's embrace, and holding up his hand.

Y

'Hark, do you hear? There's the passing bell. . . .'

No suspicion had crossed his mind. It
was a familiar sound to the Rectory child.

'Listen, Uncle John!' he said eagerly.
'Let us count, and then we shall know how
old the person is who has just gone to
Heaven. We always do, when we hear it.
Hush! don't speak, or I shall make a
mistake. Two! . . . there it goes again!
Three! . . .'

John Ramsay lost his presence of mind
altogether, and said not a word.

He sat as if turned to stone, with his
gaze fixed upon the child's face; framing
words and sentences in his head to say
when the bell should have told its tale.

And so the two remained opposite each
other, each in a listening attitude; the old
man bolt upright, in a stiff, strained posi-

tion almost paralysed with repressed emotion ; the child full of eager attention, his
earnest eyes raised to his uncle's, his lips
apart, and his hand lifted !

Four ! . . .

Five ! . . .

Six ! . . .

Seven ! . . .

Past twenty now ! . . . past thirty ! .
past forty ! . . . past forty-five. . . . A
mist comes over John Ramsay's eyes. He
closes them, and his grasp on the chair is
tightened. His head swims, he loses count
for a moment ; the words and sentences
gallop, and mingle in wild confusion in his
head.

He opens his eyes with a start, thinking
the moment must have come.

Gillie is still standing in the same attitude, still eagerly counting.

It seems to John Ramsay as if for years he has been sitting there, stringing words and sentences together, and for years Gillie has been standing in front of him, counting, counting!

He is roused by the sound of the child's voice.

' Past eighty-two now, Uncle John, and the bell still going on!' . . .

At the same moment the door opens, and Mrs. Pryor enters, joy beaming in her eyes and working in every feature.

' The message from the Rectory has come, sir,' she exclaims: ' the Rector has got safely through the night, and the doctor has pronounced him out of danger.'

There is an exclamation of delight from Gillie as he springs towards Mrs. Pryor, with the eager cry: ' Is he quite, *quite* well again? Oh! when may I go and see him?'

and the sound of the good woman's en-
dearing response as she covers the child
with kisses.

But there is no other sound in the room.

John Ramsay neither moved nor spoke.

He got up presently, slowly and feebly
from his chair, and tottered out of the
room.

The tension and then the sudden relief
had been too much for him ; and when he
reached the library he bowed his head on
his shaking hands, and sobbed and cried
like a child.

CHAPTER III.

AN INTERVIEW.

On a sofa near the open window, in all the weakness of early convalescence, Gilbert Ramsay was lying.

He was quite alone.

He was lying there in his weakness and his depression, thinking over his position, and trying to realise it: thinking sadly of his strength sapped, and his work come to an end.

It required all his faith and all his submission to face and to bow to the prospect before him.

His health was, for the time, wrecked.

He was thrown back months in his work : his income could not stand the strain which had been put upon it, and his home was uninhabitable.

He and his family, the doctor said, must remove. It was imperative that they should do so.

And he himself must have change, rest, leisure, and other impossibilities, for many months.

All this had dawned upon him recently. He had been too ill to know much till now ; too weak to be allowed to worry himself with thought of any kind.

But convalescence had now thoroughly set in, and the future must, and *would*, be thought out.

There was nothing now to hinder the rush of sad and depressing thoughts which were sweeping over him.

For the moment they overpowered
him.

It was just then that a maid entered
softly, and said that Mr. Ramsay from the
Manor-House was below, and wished to
know if he would see him.

The sick man visibly shrank into himself.

He recoiled from the thought for a
moment. He felt he could hardly bear it.
A feeling of repugnance came over him,
with which he felt powerless to contend.

'I *cannot*,' he said to himself. He
knew of course nothing that had passed
all this time: not even that his brother
had been living at the Manor-House. He
knew his little boy to be with Mrs. Pryor,
and he knew nothing further.

His brother meant to him only the
John Ramsay of that painful and dis-

appointing interview; and later on the John Ramsay who had totally ignored his appeal for help in averting the calamity which had since overwhelmed him.

He had been willing for long to think the best of his brother, and to put the most charitable construction on his behaviour.

He had tried to give him credit for not having received, for having overlooked, or for not having taken in, the importance of his original communication. So after an interval he had written again, a more urgent letter than the first.

But when that second appeal met with the same treatment at his brother's hands he could deceive himself no longer.

He was forced to realise, however unwillingly, that his only blood-relation cared no more for him and his children than if they had been utter strangers; and that he was what he had half-suspected during their interview in London, a hard, cold, worldly, self-absorbed, miserly man.

There was no other conclusion to be drawn.

To a man like Gilbert Ramsay, who had lived so long *in* and *for* others: who had long ago dedicated his life to the service of his Master, which meant to the service of his fellow-men, this state of feeling was almost incomprehensible.

That state of insensibility to the affairs and feelings of others, in which it becomes at last an impossibility to detach yourself from yourself, and to throw yourself into other people, was to him unknown; he could not understand it. His brother and his brother's conduct were to him sealed books of an unfathomable mystery.

But he was a man of great toleration, and of unbiassed judgment. He could always look on both sides of a question, and give each its due weight, even where it conflicted with his own view of the case.

He had, in the large manufacturing town in which he had spent half his life, come across every kind of character; and his knowledge of human nature was derived, not from books, but from the study of the living model itself.

He was always ready to make allowance for extenuating circumstances. It was not in his nature to condemn any one unheard.

It was only for a few moments, therefore, that these feelings of repugnance overcame him.

His brother might still be able to explain away his conduct. His higher nature prevailed, and he said, very quietly, 'Bring Mr. Ramsay up.'

There was a short interval, and then the door was opened, and John Ramsay advanced to his brother's side.

Both were shy and constrained. Gilbert held out his hand, and John took it in silence.

Then, in a few faltering words, John Ramsay said what he had long made up his mind to say: told his brother how bitterly he regretted his conduct, and asked his forgiveness. Clearly this was not what Gilbert had expected.

He looked up surprised, and the brothers' eyes met; they gazed at each other.

Something in the softened expression of the face he was looking at, struck the sick man, and he exclaimed: 'Why John! you look a different man to when I saw you last!'

John Ramsay's lips were unlocked now.

'All the child,' he said huskily; and then in answer to his brother's wondering, puzzled look of enquiry, in a voice which faltered at first, but grew stronger as he went on, he told his tale—told how the pure influence of a beautiful little life, lived out daily before him in all its simplicity, all its earnestness, all its guile-lessness, all its love and charity, had humanised him, softened him, raised him.

He painted vividly the state in which he had been previously living, heart, soul, and spirit, dead and buried—from which hideous incarceration the child had been the means of releasing him.

And he ended by begging his brother to show his forgiveness by allowing him to do anything and everything that was in his power for the future, both for himself and his family.

And then he waited for his answer.

Gilbert Ramsay did not give it for some time.

He turned his head away to hide the tears that rose into his eyes.

He was more moved than he could almost bear in his present state of physical weakness by the thought of his child, and of all that that child had been the instrument, in God's hands, of accomplishing.

For a few minutes he could think of nothing else.

But he controlled his thoughts with a strong effort, for that was not, for the moment, the point on which he wished them to dwell. He continued to gaze thoughtfully out of the window, but his face grew calmer, and the current of his thoughts flowed into another channel. He was accustomed, as we said just now, to put himself (metaphorically) into other people's places, and to try to see things from their point of view ; knowing well that from that standpoint other people's difficulties look very different to what they do from your own.

He was doing this now. He was trying to put himself into his brother's place at the time when his conduct seemed so heart-less, so incomprehensible.

What had so puzzled and saddened him began to be more comprehensible. There came upon him a vivid realisation of the state of utter desolation in which that brother had, according to his own showing, been living : the deeps and the darkness in which his heart and soul had been sunk.

He seemed to see it all with a flash.

A man, who had quenched the Spirit, and was living with no hope, and without God in the world.

He had wondered much, but he wondered no longer.

It all stood out clear.

He raised his eyes to his brother's face, and held out his hand, saying, 'I see it all now: I understand.' And, he added, in a lower tone, as he took his brother's hand in his own still feeble grasp, '*Tout comprendre, c'est tout pardonner!*'

JOHN RAMSAY

Z

CLOSING CHAPTER.

JOHN RAMSAY.

MANY years have passed away since, the interview recorded in the preceding chapter; and I will ask you to take a farewell glance at John Ramsay, ere we leave him, sitting in the library, to-night.

That a long period has elapsed is evident, for he holds in his hands a letter from an Oxford undergraduate, signed with Gillie's name.

John Ramsay's face is much altered, since we first saw him sitting in that very place, on the night of his arrival at home; sitting, weary and dispirited, looking out upon an empty life and an aimless future. The weary, unsatisfied look has gone for ever; a very different expression reigns in its stead.

Though there is even greater power and determination in the face than there used to be, there is that blending of strength and tenderness which harmonise so beautifully together.

Life makes the countenance.

The expression alters in later years, as the soul or self within becomes more formed, more definite; and looks out, as it were, through the face.

And John Ramsay's wears a spiritualised expression, which used not to be there.

Let us guess at his inner history since we saw him last.

He had feared, as we know, that when

the child was taken from him, the old hardness and indifference would return.

But just as with those who die; so with those from whom we are parted— ' the charm increases when sight is changed for memory, and the changeful irritation of time, for changeless recollection and regret.' [1]

There is left us a ' mystic presence that can never fade.'

And so it was with our Enceladus. Midas had left a golden light behind him, which neither time nor change could dull, nor any other thing extinguish.

The child was gone ; the contemplation of the little life of guileless innocence was no longer daily before him ; but the influence of its peace and of its purity remained.

It abode with John Ramsay still.

[1] *Little Schoolmaster Mark.*—Shorthouse.

And though no child dies so completely as the child who lives to grow up; yet the memory of the child of that three weeks' companionship never really left him.

It was a possession for ever.

But John Ramsay had not stopped there. The terrible consequences of his original selfishness had taught him a great lesson.

They had given him a horror of the *state* of selfishness in which he had been sunk, from which the indirect act had, as a matter of course, sprung; for it is from what we *are* that what we *do* flows as naturally as possible.

'We prepare ourselves,' says Tito, 'for sudden deeds, by the reiterated choice of good and evil, which gradually determines character.'

His sin, he saw, was in the *being* what he *was*; and his aim became *to be* something very different.

It was not all done in a moment, and he went through much mental trouble on his way.

The memory of the sermon he had listened to in the old county-town, when the planted seed of the child's influence had been watered and vivified, came back to his assistance.

And yet the thought of the capabilities which every man's life contains, as then pointed out to him, had at first been all sad and depressing.

For he had said to himself that it was all very well for others, but too late for him; that *his* life lay all behind him, a dim vista of wasted years, lived with no holy purpose, devoid of any noble aim.

Downcast at this thought, and at the shortness of the time before him, he had been well-nigh in despair ; till he had re-called to himself the man 'who, in his dying moments, gathered up the fragments of a lifetime by the intensity of one aspiration, and is to-day with Christ, for ever, in the Paradise of God.'

Then had arisen in his mind the firm resolution to gather up the fragments that remained that nothing be lost. He saw that even at the eleventh hour there were capabilities to be made use of; and that God would accept the remnant of a life—poor and unworthy though it might be.

To this resolution he brought all the strength of his whole heart and nature; that concentration and that absorption which were such marked features in his character, and which had hitherto been given so exclusively to an unworthy end.

The Result? . . .

How shall I tell of it? How put it into prose? How can I speak of the divine radiance shed around the path of one who 'does justly, loves widely, and walks humbly with his God?'

Such a life is a poem in itself. Its Heaven has half begun.

His human sympathies awoke within him and began to flow forth in love and goodwill to all around, turning everything he touched into gold.

He entered daily into deeper and deeper meanings of the axiom that 'to love is to go out of self.'

New views of life and its meaning came upon him; and to make the world around him, in the niche allotted to him,

better, and happier, became his lifelong
endeavour.

He saw, that while he was searching
for his past recollections, for the ' Heaven
that lay around him in his infancy,' God
had been leading him on to something
better worth having; and that it was *this*,
which he had really wanted, all the
thne l

'Such are the feelings,' says Newman,
' with which men look back upon their
childhood. . . . They are full of affection-
ate thoughts towards their first years, but
they do not know why. They think it is
those very first years which they yearn
after, whereas it is the presence of God,
which, as they now see, was then over
them which attracts them. They think they
regret the past, when they are but longing
after the future. It is not that they would

be children again: but that they would be angels, and would see God.'

John Ramsay realised that

> Not only round us in our infancy
> Doth Heaven with all its splendour lie.

So his cry is no longer 'Never grow up, Gillie, always remain as you are!' He knows now that he need not have feared and dreaded so much to see the child's youth and innocence pass away.

He can bear now to see him leaving the golden gates of his childhood behind him, and advancing across the plains of life: because he knows there is something in front of him grander than the mere innocence of youth.

Beautiful as it was, in its way, there is a possibility before him more beautiful still.

The innocence must go, the light must fade from the paradise of childhood; but only to make room for something higher, and more enduring.

It is neither possible, nor wise, nor even desirable, to prolong the days of innocence.

It—like many other things that are beautiful in their place, and in their order— becomes unlovely by forced, or undue, prolongation. It is only fitted to early years. Every age has its beauty and fitness, if people would only believe it.

And so, in the joy of Gillie's opening and developing life, John Ramsay finds ample comfort and absorption.

He does not expect it to be all easy, for he has realised that just as the highest good is often only to be obtained through suffering, so to the highest state of perfection the road often lies through battles waged and conquests won.

He is prepared, and content withal, to

see Gillie through struggles, through
failures, through *falls* even, if it must be so;
ever aiming at, though ever falling short of,
that holiness which is so far above mere innocence; and something of which is, even
here, possible of attainment to those who
really and persistently seek it.

. . . . . .

And yet there are times, for all that,
when John Ramsay is glad to put aside
the thought of the present and the future,
and to let memory bring back to him the
thought of the past.

Sitting alone in the library, gazing into
the fire, his thoughts will stray back sometimes to the beginning of it all: to the time
when the touch of the small, coaxing hands
upon his knees, the wistful brown eyes gazing up into his face, had first awakened the
dormant feelings of love and tenderness

within him; to those old days, long ago, when, wandering about in the June sunlight, hand-in-hand with his child-guide, his eyes had been opened to see that in the world around him, and in those about him, to which they had long been closed; when the eye of faith had begun to see clearly, and the power of realising the Unseen been bestowed; when, in a word, his long-buried spirit had been called to life, and he had entered the kingdom of Heaven—led by a little child.

THE END.

G & C.

PRINTED BY
SPOTTISWOODE AND CO., NEW-STREET SQUARE

Lightning Source UK Ltd.
Milton Keynes UK
UKHW020535260119
336225UK00011B/692/P